LAURA LEE BAHR

a division of Eraserhead Press

Copyright

© 2011 Laura Lee Bahr. All rights are reserved. No part of this book may be used or reproduced in print, electronically, or otherwise without express written consent of the author, with the exception of brief quotations embedded in articles and reviews.

This book is a work of fiction. The characters, incidents, and dialogues are products of the author's imagination and are not to be construed as real. Any resemblance to actual events or persons living or dead is entirely coincidental.

ISBN 1-936383-89-6

Cover photo by Maria Fulmer
Author photo by Brad C. Wilcox
Layout, design and typesetting by Paula Rozelle Hanback

Dedication

This is for you.

Acknowledgements

Skipp, for everything.

Bizarro-in-Chief Rose O'Keefe, for saying yes.

Mom, for letting me come home again. Shannon, for the blood-stone.

The Nappies, for knowing how to show a lady a good time.

Dear friends who read it — or tried to — in its past incarnation. Ezra, for direction when it was lost. Carolynne, for clarity. Natasha, for loving it so. Zoe, for guidance. Paula Rozelle Hanback for laying it all out. Maria Fulmer for covering me with your perfect shadow.

And again, Skipp, really — everything.

And Simon, who found me in the darkness and whispered in my ear the way out. It was just so crazy it worked.

CURSE OF THE HAUNTING FUNGASM
A THOUGHTFUL INTRODUCTION BY
JOHN SKIPP

SO YOU'RE READING THIS MANUSCRIPT that somebody handed you—something you did not expect to be reading—and you find yourself thinking, fuck, this is wonderful. I don't know where to put it, exactly, on the literary flow chart, but I love that about it! And you get all excited.

There aren't too many books that seem to do what this is doing. You think of *The Dice Man* by Luke Rhinehart (real name, George Cockcroft). You think of *Fight Club*. You think of *Catch-22*. You think about *Valis*-era Philip K. Dick, and *Even Cowgirls Get the Blues*.

But more than these books—these entirely unrelated books, which all tickle at pieces of what you're reading, conceptually or stylistically, but really aren't like it at all—you find yourself thinking about movies you've seen. Movies that also didn't fall into any neat categorization.

Movies like Lynch's *Mulholland Drive*, or Kaufman and Gondry's *Eternal Sunshine of the Spotless Mind*. Movies that fall under Video Watchdog writer Michael Barrett's definition of "Millennial Unreality Films". Which is to say: movies that no longer trust in consensus reality, and suggest that *life* really is but a dream, sliding out from under us whenever the hell it pleases.

These are movies that many people love and swear by, despite (or because of) their inability to be sold to you in normative terms. But which nonetheless cut to the heart of this relentlessly weirdening era.

People love them because they're weird, and challenging, and brilliant, but also entertaining and satisfying on a startling number of levels.

You feel like you're starting to close in on what this book is, and how it makes you feel.

Now suppose that you are me.

What do you do, when a manuscript like this gets dropped in your lap? Do you try to figure out what publisher on Earth might buy this, taking a crazy chance that their marketing department might somehow know how to sell it, but guessing they wouldn't?

Do you tell the person who handed you this, "It's great, but I don't know anybody in publishing who would take a chance on it. I'm sorry," and then walk away, throwing up your arms and going whaddaya gonna do?

Or do you say, "Fuck it. I'm gonna put this out, because I think a whole lot of people will love it every bit as much as I do, given half a chance." And then give them the chance?

If you were me, you'd do the last one.

Haunt is the first book from Fungasm Press. It is, in fact, the book that forced me to form this publishing imprint, as a place to put incredible books I love, books that fit no other category but "I love this weird book, and think other people will seriously get off on it, too."

As such, I went straight to Eraserhead Press: the flagship publisher of no-holds-barred Bizarro fiction, where weirdness is the central ingredient, and heartfelt entertainment value is the key.

Bizarro is often defined as the literary equivalent of "the cult section in a really great video store". And I'd say that is accurate as hell. I'd also call it the Adult Swim of modern literature, and align it with the underground comix genius of guys like R. Crumb and Robt. Williams.

But *Haunt* doesn't operate at that level of unbridled pandemonium. It operates somewhere at the weird juncture where mainstream *New Yorker*-style literary fiction meets genre fiction (mysteries, ghost stories, noir), and then careens wildly, giddily, profoundly into the totally fucking weird, right here on Earth.

That's a Fungasm, for me.

Which brings me, at last, to Laura Lee Bahr: the woman who dropped this unexpected bomb of awesome in my lap, and whose words you are about to sink into.

She's an actress, a singer, a playwright and screenwriter. Which is to say, she's ridiculously talented. This is her first novel, which shows itself largely by breaking every rule that ordinary novels abide by, in much the same way that songwriters like Bjork both instinctively know what good popular songs do, and then naturally, idiosyncratically mutate that into cheerfully deep-yet-dangerously catchy oddball singularity.

As a person, Laura is sweet and smart and kind, incredibly lovely and fun and *funny*, yet utterly, painfully present in the moment. Which means she knows too much about who we really are, and it leaks out all over her prose, with an honesty both richly compassionate and shockingly unsparing.

She spent seven years writing this book, in between teaching, film and theater gigs. It was originally conceived as a "Choose Your Own Adventure" novel for grownups, and part of that structure still stands, although she took out the whole "Turn to Pg. 88" motif.

As such, it will yank you all over the place, like a child. Like the semi-grown-up child you are.

To tell you more would be to fuck up the surprises.

And I am not that kind of guy.

So if I were you, I'd accept this deliberately cagey introduction for just what it is: a whole-hearted endorsement of a novel I love, designed to twist you in all sorts of wondrous ways that I suspect you will enjoy.

You have never read anything like it. ME, NEITHER!

I hope you fungasm as I much as I did.

Yer pal in the trenches,
Skipp

PROLOGUE

DEAD IS DEAD. Why split hairs, nitpick or obsess over an actual cause when there are so many to choose from? It could be drowning, it could be loss of blood. Why harp on suffocation like it's an answer to a riddle?

"Wrist-cutters don't suffocate, that's why," says the detective-man, and the autopsy-man nods. The paper-man looks confused. The wrists are slit open in two huge crosses, leaving a bloody mess that makes for the obvious cause of death, and leads logically to the conclusion that this young woman committed suicide.

Drowning would also be a reasonable cause, since she was found in an overflowing bathtub. But no...?

The "actual cause," according to the man who gets the final word in actual causes, is suffocation of all things. A paper-man might thus be led to believe that this cut, naked, water-logged corpse has a few stories to tell.

But for now, the only story the corpse is telling is through the mouth of the autopsy-man, whose training in science affirms his authority to say that despite appearances to the contrary, it is "asphyxiation."

How does science tell you the difference between asphyxiation, drowning and bleeding to death?

There are people, ladies and gentlemen, whose job it is to know such things. But this is not a story about those people and their jobs.

No, friend.

It is a story about you.

It is a story that is told as most stories are, "*this* and then *that*." But unlike most stories, it is told as if you could see how *if* you had done *that* instead of *this*, what you would have got *there*.

Because as you may or may not know, different actions lead to different consequences but seldom the ones you would suppose.

I tell it to you like *this*, always happening now—"you do *this* and *that* happens or you do *this* instead and something else happens"— because that is how I see it now, here, where I am.

Where I am is very different from where you are.

Where I am, I no longer have illusions of this or that leading me anywhere at all.

I tell you plainly that this corpse was mine.

There are many things I once thought of as mine that no longer belong to me.

Your apartment, for example.

Who are you?

PART ONE – LEAVING THINGS BEHIND

Wherein...

Sarah may or may not take up smoking.

You leave the couch outside.

We all wonder what it is about this Simon character.

YOU

WHOEVER YOU ARE, YOU ARE ALONE.

Sadness spills out and over you and you feel you might weep. It seems this emotion itself echoes into a song that vibrates throughout the room. The moment itself is singing—a minor key song, distant yet clear, of aching beauty, love found and lost, and an eternity of longing. Then you remember that you are not alone, after all. You have a ghost to keep you company... but you are sleeping, still.

Keep sleeping.

You dream you are in a place (your place, but it is different, not your place as it is now. Was this your place when it was hers?) filled with strange light that keeps changing: white to blue to sepia. A young woman sits on the couch. She is very pretty but strange and frightening in a way you can't quite identify. Maybe it is the way her eyes keep changing colors or that the smoke from her cigarette is not moving. It is stuck, as if the air is glue.

She is smiling at you. The light is white.

"Yes, I know," she says to you, but you have said nothing to her.

You feel desperate; you have some all-important message for her. You rack your brain and you suddenly say it: "You're dead."

The light in the room is blue.

The cigarette is suddenly whole and unlit, and she is snapping her fingers as if that could spark it.

"We have met before," she says, "though I'm not sure we were formally introduced."

You've had enough. She is sitting on your couch, (wait—you don't have a couch) in your room, and she starts to fade feet first like the Cheshire Cat.

"Who are you?" you say.

"You dreamt it backwards," she says, as only her eyes gleam, changing to match the hazy sepia of the room. "Go the other way, now." And she disappears.

A long, loud, painful sound—a buzz that extends and you reach for recognition. The phone is ringing. It is a startling sound snap-pulling you through layers of consciousness. It is a sound that demands response. You pick it up, unsure of who you are and a voice reminds you.

"Richard Jamison?" says a voice you do not recognize. Is it her? Your ghost?

"Yes?" you say. You are awake now. It is morning, and today looks like the same place you left last night when you fell asleep—only brighter.

"Mr. Jamison," the voice continues, "are you getting the most from your cable service?"

No, you really aren't. You are sure you actually could be getting more. You have a long conversation with the robotic woman and at the end of it, you are getting many, many more channels than you will ever watch and giving a nice commission to a robot lady that will make her day. You are quite a giver.

Yes, you are. And you say so. As you click down on the receiver you remember that you do not believe in ghosts, nor are you interested in believing in them. The sadness and the loneliness and the dream and the ghost are all obliterated the moment you convince yourself of your own existence.

Who are you?

Why, of course you know. You are Richard Jamison, "Rich, please" of the Kansas City, Missouri, Jamisons. Check out that mirror. Yes, you are rather hot; and if you do say so yourself, you aren't the only one. Blue eyes. Dark blonde hair to match your dark blonde pubes. Skin the color of whole milk. You need a tan, but you can't get one. You have a large angular nose and an Adam's apple so huge that when paired with your head you make a double-dip cone. It bobs on a beat when you speak, in a strident tone that means business. You wear nice clothes. You wear nice briefs. You wear cologne that attracts chicks because it smells of money. You are sane, clever and callow. You are only 26 years old. You also have your health.

Congratulations.

Your name for your cock is "number one." You have never performed oral sex on any of your girlfriends because you find it, frankly, disgusting. You believe you are a "man's man." You are right.

You like popular music. You have a nice stereo. You think "it's all good."

Your spirituality is reserved for music, for which you have an insatiable desire to participate. You want to be a rock star, but you don't have the chops to live in your own filth. So, you settle for being a ballad man. You have a surprisingly rough and sexy singing voice that you can bust out for the girls you bring back to your place. You will sing them Hendrix, Beatles, Pearl Jam, Nirvana. You are working on writing your own music (painful) here in California, where you have recently moved from Kansas City to "make it."

"Making it" means making compromises, which necessitate a tolerable enough day-job in the Business Development Office of Brighton Research. You make a respectable five figures—especially since you are a recently minted MBA with fair-to-middling grades. Again, congrats.

Your apartment is located in the under-gentrification district in Venice, California. Its main attributes are affordable rent, high ceilings, large windows and a five minute walk to the beach. Its main draw-backs are the occasional rat-a-tat-tat of gunshots, the faulty electricity, the neighbors, and that the five-minute walk to the beach is a freak show. (Oh, and also that it is haunted. You tend not to notice such things, though, when you are conscious).

This morning is a gray morning. Children count backwards and end with "blast-off" outside your window.

After your shower and tea, you sit in a lotus pose and ask what your country can do for you. You think that if you become a rich and famous musician, you will become enlightened. Enlightened enough, anyway. For this you pray, though you do not believe in God. You are clever enough to realize that you need some divine intervention, or at least some divine networking. You rise from your knees and sit down in your living room with your guitar. It doesn't matter what you play. It's shit.

In this apartment a minor tornado of supernatural energy flips your bedroom light off and on, off and on. You don't notice. You are, after all, in the living room.

But enough about you. Let's talk about my problems with you:

I don't like the way you keep the apartment. No pets, no real friends except a couple of infrequent lame-wads who watch weekly sit-coms and never spill their beers. You don't have a couch, so maybe that's why you don't have any friends. You drink like a pussy. I knock shit over and open the cupboards while you're at work. I wish I could smoke and leave cigarettes burning for you to find when you come home, but that is a rather difficult task. I'm working on it, though.

You are working on looking less like a tool but only looking more like a tool, putting product in your hair and finding far too attractive that man in the mirror. Ugh. You are working on walking out the door.

I think you should work on giving people a place to sit. There is a couch right outside your apartment. You don't need to know where it came from; it's there right now. It's lovely—a sky blue with intricate gold leaves and real oak armrests and back. It isn't quite in keeping with your character, but like I said, you are going to have to change your character to make friends, and a musician needs all the fake and real friends he can cajole or conjure. Whaddya say?

Do you leave it?

—Or—

Do you know that a couch precedes friends and take it?

SIMON WOULD

YOU TAKE TRASH *OUT*, NOT *IN*.

You leave the couch with barely a second glance. Off to the day job.... where....

HEY! You have been staring off into space again. People will think your heart isn't in it: sitting at your cubicle, between puke-gray carpet and puke-white rectangles as migraine-inducing flores-cent lights inch closer and closer to your crown daily. You work in a small animal box—you have a sudden uninvited image of a hamster you brought home as a child, with its nose twitching through a hole for breathing. There are no such holes here.

You are suddenly out of breath and walk outside for air. Outside it is hot and the gray morning has turned blindingly bright. You proceed with a constitutional around the block.

A man stands on the sidewalk, smoking with strange gesticula-tions for something that is assumedly habitual. He is an odd-looking fellow, a strange color between brown and gray, his dark hair coming out of his head like a tightly-packed helmet sprouting single curls. Odd-looking in the good-looking sort of way, if he didn't appear so sickly.

He wears a red-striped shirt, his pants hang off him like a bag on a string and his sneakers have holes. He may be homeless. He may ask you for money. In fact, he is limping, yes limping towards you.

You cross the street to pass him, walking faster.

"Do you work here?" he calls after you, in a voice that has the husky, deep, desperation of a spurned lover.

You scarcely turn, and he is upon you. He has blocked your continuation down the sidewalk, his cigarette cupped in his palm in a way that must burn him, but no, his palm is cupped open and smoke from the cherry lifts up through the other side.

"I'm sorry?" you say.

"Don't you work at Brighton Research?" he asks, flipping the cigarette out of his palm to inhale and then back in, in repose.

"Yes, but I haven't been there very long yet."

"Just wait," he says. "Twenty years and you'll get the pewter paperweight."

"You work at Brighton?"

"Indeed. About twenty days. In twenty years, I'll be dead."

You aren't sure whether to laugh or what, so you just stare at him. He pushes out his un-smoking hand as if to keep himself from falling, but holds the pose so long you see he wants to shake.

You hold his hand in yours. Your hand is warm and moist, his dry and cold but it shakes firm and holds.

"Simon Would. What do they pay you to do?"

Bells start ringing at his name. You knew him before, you see, you go way back, back so far you blink your eyes and wait for the incoming data... which you may receive or not, depending how quickly you open your mouth.

You wait for it.

Flashback to grade three and the new kid who was darker than the other kids and spoke funny. You stayed in the library for recess when you had a cold and he was there, a recess regular, with stacks of open encyclopedias that he closed when you approached. You asked him what he was reading and he smiled and said he was "doing research." You asked him what that was, see you didn't know, and he said, "finding everything you can about something before you do it."

You were friends, sort of, spending some recesses together playing make-believe... and you got in trouble, you can't exactly remember how or why. He moved at the end of the year. A deep discomfort is buried beneath all that, like guilt or shame if you could name it, as if he were sent away and you were an accomplice (to what? You can't remember. It had never made sense to you anyway, only to him). He moved, you heard, to some distant sprawling city.

Maybe it was this very sprawling city, where you have now found him.

"Simon!" you say, slapping his shoulder like an old drinking buddy, though last time you saw him you still wet the bed. "It's me! Richard Jamison!"

He feigns complete recognition. "Dick?"

"Rich. Or Richard." He nods. "Still doing research, I see," you say, thinking of the encyclopedias. "Remember?" you say. "The library?"

"Of course," he says. "You made it out of Dubuque, I see."

You've never even been to Dubuque. "Did you live in Dubuque?"

you query politely.

"I was being metaphorical, metaphorical, old chum." He puts an arm around you and throws down the cigarette.

You laugh, unsure if he actually does remember you. Perhaps you've made a mistake somewhere, now feeling the entirety of your body pulse with something electric at his embrace. "So, whatever happened to you? I knew you moved away, but..."

"I moved here. That's what happened to me." Simon answers.

You nod affably. You pride yourself in being universally affable.

"Well!" you say. "Life is certainly full of surprises!" Often you say very stupid things.

You turn and walk away.

He does you the discourtesy of following.

"I could show you around, you know," he continues. "This is my city. Are you new here?"

"No." It's a lie.

"All right then," he says. He stops and you keep walking.

"Oh—just a little friendly heads up," he says in a musical change of tone, calling from behind you. "Don't get freaked out if you see her."

"See who?" you say.

"The ghost," he says.

"The *ghost*?" you repeat, with all possible ridicule.

"Yeah, you'll see her sometime, if you play it right."

You stare at him. Is there a smile on his lips, or is it just the simpering of someone cracked?

"Don't get freaked out," he says, calmly, coolly, "if you see her."

And he runs the other way in a broken dash.

SARAH'S BOYFRIEND

YOU WALK BACK INTO WORK from the sunlight, blinking with the transition and keeping an over-the shoulder lookout for Simon. He frightens you, and you would just as soon avoid him at all costs.

You purchased a smoothie—strawberry with protein powder—on your walk about the block and are sucking it loudly as you stop by the cubicle of your favorite of the assistants, Sarah. She is sending an e-mail and is obviously embarrassed to be caught not working as you look over her shoulder.

"Hi," she says, blushing, closing the window of her e-mail.

"That your boyfriend?" you ask, noting a cut out clipping pasted to Sarah's PC. It is a dark man with dark eyes—handsome—you've seen him somewhere before. Something stirs in your stomach and you feel a little sick, too much smoothie, maybe.

"Oh, I wish," says Sarah. "I got this from GQ. They did this spread about... what did they call it? 'Hot writers in hot fashions'—he was at a Charity Cake-Walk wearing this. Doesn't he look dreamy?"

You put your ass against her desk and stare at the opposite direction as if bored.

"Do anything interesting this weekend?" you ask her.

"Um, yeah—just partied, you know."

You like Sarah because she's cute, she's sweet, and she doesn't wear a bra. You are the same age as she is, have similar aspirations (you found out in the break-room that she wants to be a singer), and you make probably double what she makes and at some point, when you are a little more comfortable with your way around here, you can ask her to make you copies and collate your reports.

She is, you are intuitively aware, far "too cool" for you, but you still might ask her to get a drink with you after work, someday. You steal a look at her nipples, hard against her shirt. You imagine reaching your hand to the one on the right, pinching it, squeezing it, sucking it—it's practically begging you to do it. Instead you suck your straw and pat her shoulder, standing up to move back to your office.

"By the way," you say, "do you know Simon Would?"

She laughs so loudly, so close to hysterically, that you actually tell her to "shush."

"Sorry," she says. "That's funny."

"You do?" you whisper, not wanting to start the laugh riot again.

"You mean Simon Would, my hot 'boyfriend'?" she says, with her eyes sparking and mischievous and obvious quotes around the 'boyfriend' part like it was a joke at a bar.

Is she making fun of him? Is she making fun of his limping, homeless look? That doesn't seem like her humor. But then again, do you really know her? Is Simon really her boyfriend? Is she really dating this clearly-cuckoo guy in baggy pants?

Unsure, you ask. "You think Simon Would is 'hot'?"

Now she looks offended. She rolls her eyes at you and opens her e-mail again. "Duh," she says, without looking at you again.

You think about telling her you went to grade school with Would. Will this up your cred with her?

It most certainly will. Wait for it. Get a drink in her first.

Don't forget number one, Dick. It's been a dry couple of months. Back home, you were a stud. Here, you're a wannabe and a tool.

You don't really have a choice. She's ignoring you now.

Wait for it.

WANNA GET LUCKY?

YOU WALK BACK TO YOUR OFFICE, sucking your smoothie and feeling all... shivers down your spine. Usually smoothies cause brain-freeze. A strange idea comes to you, that shivers down the spine maybe once made all the hair stand up on the human animals' back—like a cat, maybe making it more frightening to that which frightened it. Evolution, baby.

It comes to you, unwelcome. The memory you weren't looking for:

Simon Would has a serious complex. He has no perception of people as dead because his mother died when he was young and thus he cannot and will not ever actually accept that she is not somewhere where she can hear and see him.

You remember now that he was convinced then, in 3rd grade, that he could find a tunnel to her exact location. That was his research—that is how you got in trouble—he had removed slats in the library ceiling and you helped him climb up. He was trying to find her, his dead mother, in the ceiling of the school library!

You have no hair on your back; shivers still go up and down your spine.

Lewis, your co-worker, slaps you five. "What's so funny?" he asks.

"What?" you say.

"Heard you laughing over there," he says.

"Oh—just. Nothing," you say, thinking you have no idea what Sarah was even laughing at.

"Big meeting at 2:00. You checked your e-mail?" Lewis asks. You sit at your desk and shiver a little. They keep this office freezing. Must have an enormous AC bill. Not your problem, but you wish you had a sweater. You feel exhausted. You should have got an energy boost instead of a protein boost in that smoothie.

You open your e-mail to see something from Sarah.

to: ricjimmy@brigtonbeach.com
from: sarawillie@brightonbeach.com
Subject: Wanna Get Lucky?
Date: 03/13/01

Message:

Will I see you tonight? SW

This is why she was blushing. Now you're blushing. Now number one is blushing. Bam! You still got the touch! Short wait, my friend.

Now, you just get that drink in her, tell her your Simon connection and it's a done deal. She is definitely not dating him. Or she is a slut. Wait. Should you? Do you really wanna mess with another guy's girl? But what could she possibly see in that guy. Maybe she's trying to trade up? You read it again, slowly. "Wanna get lucky?" Damn right, sweet tits! You are gonna tap that ass of hers so hard, that little fucking slut! Telling you Simon's her boyfriend knowing she just asked you to come over tonight and fuck her brains out... Course, the date's all wrong. That's the first thing — that was well over a year ago. She must have been so flustered she wrote the wrong date and time. Damn — she must really like you!

You would walk back over there, but you really shouldn't stand up just yet.

You hit the "Reply" button:

"You want to get a beer after work?" you type. You hit send.

You immediately delete the e-mail she sent to you; you don't know how far it's gonna go, but if it goes as far as you want it to go, you could both get fired.

Now, although number one insists there is no more pressing matter, you have to get ready for your 2:00 meeting.

New message.

You open it, your heart jumping in expectation of a "yes" from Sarah. Instead, it's an automatic message from I.T. saying "unrecognizable address, mail undeliverable" and your message:

"You want to get a beer after work?"

It is absurd since you just hit reply and she sent YOU the message, but what are you going to do? Call I.T. and let them in on the secret?

You'll wait until number one is less someone you'd call Woody or Rocky (you make yourself laugh) and then you'll just go over to her desk, get a good look at what you'll get a better look at later.

You pull your pants and look up to see Lewis, half-smiling at you in your doorway. He knocks on your open door.

"Hey, man," says Lewis.

"What's up?" you say.

"I wanted to ask you if you have the numbers ready for the meeting at 2:00."

"Yeah, yeah. One second." You make a show of staying seated, picking up papers, picking up other papers. "Oh, I'll just print out another copy."

"You want to e-mail it to me?"

"I think my e-mail is having a little trouble. You want to pick it up off the printer?"

"Sure, man." Lewis turns to leave.

"Hey," you say. "Lewis, do you know a guy named... um, Simon? Simon Would?"

Lewis nods, thoughtfully. "Yeah, man. I know who he is."

"What's the haps on him?"

Lewis gives you a pained look. "Well, off the record?"

"Oh, yeah. Definitely."

"He ain't got long, man."

"He's dying?"

Lewis laughs. "Yeah."

You aren't sure why he's laughing since death is no laughing matter, but Lewis slaps your arm.

"Just kidding! No, no, I mean, he's gonna get laid off."

Simon, it turns out, was hired six months ago as the Chief Manager of the Writing Department, a title they made up for him since he was a "famous writer."

He was to be quite a feather in the cap of Brighton, since writers of his caliber never deigned to work for corporations such as theirs; but he was insistent that he wanted to work for Brighton, as a lowly copywriter, if necessary. They insisted it was not necessary and invented a title and a position for him.

He has since under-whelmed everyone day by day, week by week, month by month until his responsibilities are none but lowly copy-writing and being a painful reminder that his title, pay-scale, and type of employment needed to be appropriately "down-sized." None of the brass-ballers have big enough or brass enough balls to tell someone who has written for right and wrong coasts' *Times* that it is his time to go.

They feel sorry for him, for one thing. He has a drinking problem, his wife has left him and he limps. No one knows what the hell happened to him but they are afraid to ask, like they might catch it. He spends most of his time at Brighton, which isn't much time at all, sweating profusely in some strange pose at his desk or outside chain-smoking. His days are numbered, probably a number less than you have on your two hands.

You wanna ask more—you wanna ask if he knows if Simon is dating Sarah—but you don't want to tip your hand. You are definitely gonna fuck that girl tonight and you don't want to get fired over it.

WEEKLY MEETING

THE WEEKLY WEDNESDAY MEETING always makes Sarah's head swim like she is tripping on some skank weed laced with crank.

Her friend and fellow assistant, Tamara, always passes the time passing notes and making snide side comments to Lewis, the department manager but assistant-sympathizer.

The meeting usually involves sales tips, a numbers report, call challenges, policy clarifications, and bits of soft gossip. She doodles a tree—the only doodle she does that really looks like what she intended it to be—in the margin of her legal pad. The tree has infinite branches in every direction, always continuing, always reaching underlining words like corporate-tool alphabet fruit: "Client" and "Credit" and "This Week's Challenge."

She fantasizes about the day she will quit. It will not be soon enough. She fantasizes about stepping up on the table, taking off her shirt and doing a lively rendition of *"Misty."* God, she loves that song.

Maybe, for an encore, "My Funny Valentine." This morning, in the shower, she sang the national anthem, hitting the high note of "free" (as in "for the land of the...") like a pop star at a sports arena. She could hear the crowd in the water in her ears, cheering. Drugs can help with this. She could swear she heard techno-music in the pipes for weeks after her first time at a rave (and first dose of E).

She writes words on a branch as she doodles: "don't kill me this time around."

She stares a moment at this strange phrase looking up at her, and at this scene with all her co-workers, in this moment, stuck like bits of bugs in amber.

Her mind day-trips back, long before she was who she is now, past lives, to one where she was a young princess with hair, blacker than night, reaching down past her calves. Her maids spend hours brushing it. She closes her eyes remembering the weight of it. She bathes in steaming baths filled with rose-petals. It all was what it was. So few words. So many things just senses, smells, the feeling of being dressed. What country is she in? What year is it? But she is in the bath now.

Suddenly, there is someone else there. He is a revolutionary, a peasant. His eyes are black. He is hungry, bitter, wanting. What does he want? Food, justice, to possess her body?

He springs like an animal and kills her maids (two of them, her favorites). He comes to her from behind and takes her into a passionate embrace, one arm holding her head so she can see into his eyes, the other holding her naked body against him. She does not move or make a sound—her heart and her breath are held like a long note. She has never been held by a man. She has never been naked before a man. She has lived each moment before this by a series of specific traditions that she has never questioned nor resented.

He smells pungent and her nostrils widen to him. She wants to drink in the smell. He is handsome, her eyes looking deep into his black eyes with their black sun. She will not drown in them but burn. This was not planned. No one knows. Now, for the first time, she is truly alive. She is in love with him. She gasps for air and her heart pounds. What will he do?

He clits her throat.

She stares at the words in the tree, back again in this meeting, wondering who he is now. Is he someone she knows now? This lifetime?

"Sarah?"

"Yes?" She looks up from her tree with that expectant, sweet look that makes her so popular at Brighton.

The boss smiles at her. "What do you think of having a company outing to play beach volleyball?"

She smiles back and answers honestly. "I'm against it, sir."

BUBBLE WRAP

YOU WALK INTO YOUR 2:00 MEETING at precisely 2:00 (if you're early you look like you have nothing to do, late, like they have nothing to do). You are surprised to see Sarah in the back of the room, head-down and doodling on a legal pad.

She usually is not in these meetings, but maybe she's taking minutes. Maybe Tamara is sick—no, there's Tamara. Sarah doesn't look up at you, even though you make a big excuse to come close to brushing past her to get to your seat. You clear your throat, trying to get her to look up but she doesn't give you anything.

At first you are upset, but then you realize she probably is playing it cool knowing she is gonna fuck your brains out tonight. She is a smart cookie—doesn't want anyone to get an idea about what's going to go down. You'll follow her lead, and you try and make a point to avoid eye contact.

In comes the Boss, and you and Lewis deliver lines such as "our market analysis research client retention rate" and "the biz dev guys project a 32% increase in the profit margin from government agencies in the first quarter alone, sir." You deliver them better. Lewis knows this, the Boss knows it, Tamara, taking furious minutes, knows this. Only Sarah, head still down except when she turns to gaze into space, seems to have no fucking clue and breaks your focus momentarily.

What the fuck is she doing in this meeting, anyway? It occurs to you that the Boss likes her. Of course he does. Asked her to come and watch, you guess. He ignores her though.

You find yourself trying to catch her eye despite yourself, and she continues to ignore you.

When the meeting is adjourned, the Boss shakes Lewis' hand quickly, but he grabs your hand for an extended moment, looks you right in the eye to congratulate you and suggests the two of you have lunch.

Only then does he glance to Sarah's corner. By the time the Boss releases his grip, she has gone.

You make your way back to your office, past the large black plastic tarps that hang over the walls they are taking out. Company expansion. You sometimes get a good whiff of paint that would get you high as a rat if you stood there jawing to the workers. Lewis and Tamara are in Tamara's corner, hooting it up and talking in jive.

Lewis gives you a friendly hands-up sign as you pass and a "good job, man" that he doesn't mean despite the "yessir" smile on his face.

You strut yourself over to Sarah's desk. You are surprised to find it completely cleared of all personal items and the computer off. Sarah's desk wasn't the most cluttered desk you'd seen, but the G.Q. picture, a fair stack of papers and post-its seemed to disappear rather quickly. There is a piece of pink bubble-wrap on her chair.

You aren't really sure what to make of it, but you do pop three of the plastic bubbles. The popping sound alerts some temp, who puts his head over the cubicle wall. You think his name is... you have no fucking idea what his name is.

"You know where Sarah is?" you ask.

"Sorry, I'm just a temp. I don't know who Sarah is."

"Well, she sits here," you say, popping another bubble. "Did you see the girl who sits here?"

"I haven't seen anyone sitting there," he says. The temp shrugs and disappears back over the cubicle.

That Sarah is one kooky girl. Where did she disappear to?

You start to talk her down in your own mind. She's probably psycho. The psycho ones—they're the worst. They look normal, they can even be hot chicks, but you get too close and suddenly you are dealing with that chick in that movie who's boiling your baby rabbit and in your bathtub with a butcher knife. Yow. She's definitely a slut. Asking you if you wanted to get lucky. What kind of girl does that? And dating Simon?

But you can't help feeling sad. You check by her cubicle one last time on your way out, but she is gone, gone daddy gone.

SARAH

AFTER A MIND-CLAMPING DAY of setting schedules, typing memos and shredding documents, she finds herself back home with her orange tabby cats, Sergeant Tubbs and Sir Fatts. She is drinking all the alcohol she has left in the apartment—cheap tequila and rum mixed with generic cola.

Yes, it hurts.

She sings *"Misty"* and wonders where her ghost has been keeping herself. Is her ghost giving her the silent treatment or is she just paying more attention to her silence than usual because she misses her, wishes she could talk to her, see her in that glance in the mirror out of the corner of her eye, reflecting-a young ghost, a pretty ghost, who came to some tragic end and doesn't know she's dead; her own personal ghost that came with the property that she'll try to convince to leave with her when she leaves this place and... ah, she's drunk.

And there's that pack of red and gold cigarettes. Her cigarettes, apparently.

So, why not take up smoking?

There are many reasons NOT to printed on the pack, but she is too drunk to read them.

Wanna take up smoking? she asks herself in her head.

"Don't mind if I do," she says aloud.

She starts a bath with Epson salts and red bath-beads.

Drunk, smoking, she takes off her clothes. She has bruises and bites, finger marks and a palm print on her ass from birthday spankings. God. She should really be more careful, inviting total strangers into the house who slit her throat in past lives... Wait.

She struggles to grasp what is going through her mind.

"What are you thinking?" she asks herself. "What stranger? What spankings? Past-lives? What are you smoking? Since when do you smoke? *This is not you.*"

She sits in the bathtub, ashing onto the tile, pressing a hand to her third-eye chakra. Too much drinking? Too many drugs? Is this a premonition? Is this a memory from the future? Is she going to die? Does someone murder her?

She lights another cigarette successfully in spite of the facts that she is drunk, wet, and (no longer!) a non-smoker. She clears her mind and focuses on the task at hand—smoke going in, smoke going out.

The questions dissipate into wet air around her and she is glad to let them go.

It is best to not get too hung up about such details.

She's alive right now. That's what counts.

She tells herself a story, not quite sure which parts of it are true, about this character, Simon Would.

THE APPEARANCE OF
THE MEN IN SUITS

THEY ARE OUTSIDE THE APARTMENT right now.

A CAKE WALK

SARAH IS DONE FOR. First sight. She has been trying to keep her twice-broken heart on ice until it could heal, but when she sees Simon smile from across the room, its warmth melts everything in her, and her heart is dislodged in the deluge.

He is not even smiling at her, but at something amusing that is happening across the floor. A colleague of his has fallen into one of the cakes at the cake-walk. Even though the entire Gosh-Posh crowd wows at such a faux pas, she does not even notice. She can only see the brilliant white of his teeth off-set by the brown of his skin, the way his smile reaches his deep dark eyes, and the way he throws his head back with the laugh. The poor girl doesn't have a chance.

She is wearing a long pink gown that matches the pink carnation in his lapel. Whether they had met yet or not, they were clearly meant to be partners.

She is a hostess at this function, and lucky to be rubbing shoulders with the famous and generous. It is a charity cake-walk to raise money for this year's Pet Cause that has always been her cause. Her years of passionate activism won her this opportunity to smile and meet and hit up journalists, actors, singer/song-writers and television personalities for their tax-deductible donations.

Still, they are discouraged from making asses of themselves and their cause; which she will inevitably do as she feels herself being pulled closer and closer to him, her own feet walking her, as if hypnotized.

He turns his gaze toward her, acknowledging that he has effortlessly called her and yes, of course she is coming. His smile continues and he looks her in the eyes and she feels she might faint.

"Is it my turn, again?" he asks. "Now I can't fall through a cake, since Chuck already did that so beautifully. Is there one I might jump out of?"

"Huh?" Sarah is already off-balance.

"I already walked. Aren't we in the twenties, now?"

"Oh, the cake walk, you mean?"

He gives her a wink. "You do work this, don't you? Or are you just wearing that name-tag to give me an excuse to keep glancing at your tits."

She gasps and places both hands over her breasts.

"I'm just kidding. I'm just being an asshole. I mean, they are lovely and you aren't wearing a bra—but don't act so aghast, I'm just trying to make conversation, Sarah. See, I was looking at your name-tag."

She removed her hands and put one to her face. "I watch you on channel nine."

"Wonderful."

"You always have interesting commentaries."

"Thank you. It's nice to have fans."

"Oh, I'm not a fan. I've just seen you before and think you're interesting. I mean, I am a fan now, I wasn't before—I just think—oh, dear. Why can't I talk?"

"Are you drunk?"

"No, not at all."

"Well, maybe that's the problem. Want to get a drink?"

It is all happening so fast and she glances around to see if any of the Pet Cause committee members are watching. "I—uh—am not supposed to drink while I'm working."

He reaches over and pulls the name tag off her dress. He unpins the number from his lapel and carefully pins it onto her dress, his fingers lightly grazing the tips of her nipples as if by accident.

"There," he says. "I'm you and you're me. Want to blow this cake walk?"

"Well, I—"

"Now, you're me, so you have to say 'yes' because that's what I want."

Her head a bobble-head doll of yes yes yes.

"And I—let's see, what do I want? I'm you, now. And I just really need a goddamn drink without all these fuck-heads I volunteer with gawking at me, so yes—I would love to leave with this incredibly verbally adept coolly marginally famous television journalist to get a few shots of bourbon in me so I can have a polite conversation."

He slips his hand around her and walks her out like a light pink balloon on his wrist.

Outside, dark limos wait with smoking drivers. Simon doesn't wait for the door to be opened, merely walks around to the other side and opens it himself, pulling Sarah inside after him.

"Where do you live?" he whispers into her ear.

"29 Veronica Lane. Venice."

"Lovely," he says, and repeats it to the driver. "There isn't a room-mate, or someone annoying like that?" he says as an after-thought.

She shakes her head. "You aren't allergic, though? I have cats."

He has his hand up her dress and his face buried in her neck. "Sarah," he says, sliding his hand up her thigh, "I have no problems with pussies."

She half-laughs and he groans, not a pleasure moan but an embarrassed wail. He buries his head into her shoulder and then looks her in the eyes biting his lip with a half-smile.

"Sorry," he says. "Puns are my closet crack habit."

"I don't mind," Sarah says, moving his other hand to her breast. "I don't have any problem with words."

Simon instructs the driver to wait outside for him as Sarah, gig-gling compulsively, walks him up the stairs to her apartment. Bright florescent lights shine down on the white walls. Simon keeps mov-ing his hands across Sarah as they walk up the steps. When they reach her apartment door, Sarah gasps.

"I left my key—I—oh, shit—I locked the door behind me but I left my key inside."

Simon laughs, leaning against the doorway with his hands in his pockets. He is still wearing her name tag. He is drop-dead gor-geous, and Sarah puts her hand on her heart to try and slow it down. It is beating wildly, frantically, spastically, like a demon-drugged voodoo dancer.

"We can get a room somewhere," he says, smiling.

"I can break in. I just need a boost; would you mind?"

No, he did not mind at all. Already the desultory disorder of the unescorted woman's life appeals to him like a dream.

They walk around to the back staircase and he holds her up by her ass and then on his shoulders as she lifts the individual slats of glass from her second story window.

Simon feels he had never lifted any woman who had such marrow in her bones — she is surprisingly dense yet still light. She hands down several slats of glass, then instructs him to push and she rolls through the window.

"Come around," she calls and he walks back to the front door.

He realizes that he suddenly doesn't feel in control anymore. Unexpected things should be expected, especially when sleeping with new women; but as he walked around to the front, the sight of the limo already seems like a vehicle from another world (his world) that is about to trip into one unfamiliar and frightening.

The front door is open and she is sweating a little, flushed and beaming.

"May I come in?" he asks.

"Whenever you like," she says, with a grand sweep with her hand.

She runs about the apartment, turning on lights. Two well-fed orange cats regard him with sleepy eyes. Two red birds flit about a cage and a green parrot closes and opens its beak to say "Pretty bird."

The place smells sweet and warm, like he imagines hay might smell, though he has no actual experience. The walls are covered with strange cartoons, photos of Sarah with groups of people in varying stages of intoxication, green painted vines and flowers, suns, moons, stars, galaxies. It is too much to take in at once, and he feels utterly overwhelmed.

He takes off his jacket and leans against the wall. Sarah disappeared then re-appears with a half bottle of whiskey and two nearly clean glasses. She takes a slug straight from the bottle before pouring them both shots and takes hers without a shudder.

"Music. You want music?" she asks with a sing-song voice.

Off-guard, he is unsure which dimension he has stepped into. He thinks of bolting. After all, he is not hurting for play (and he is married for Christ's sake), the limo is waiting outside, and he feels suddenly, inexplicably in danger.

She has her back turned to him, she is opening a cheaply made CD player and picking through a pile of CDs and placing them aside. They remind him of coasters.

In the center of her living room floor is a typewriter.

What year is this, anyway?

She is busying herself with the music and he feels the need to make words with a just-drank-too-much-coffee-and-need-to-piss urgency.

"What's with the typewriter?" is the best he can do.

Her back is still to him as she sing-songs an answer.

"I know—I have this soft-spot for the old ways. I love the way it clicks. I used it to write letters and things."

He downs the rest of his whiskey with a face. He puts his jacket back on, peeling her name-tag off and putting it in his pocket.

Yes, he would leave now. It is time. It is past time. It is too late.

She turns around then, right as Nina Simone begins to sing "Wild is the Wind"— the most beautiful song he had ever known, a song that could always make him weep and yearn for a love he had never felt, only imagined.

It is as if it were in slow motion, as if time itself were now moving through water. She is the most beautiful, exceptional, strange looking creature he has ever seen. Her eyes fill him with something warm and trembling and his hands start shaking as she walks toward him, her eyes never leaving his, and takes them into her own.

His own voice speaks to him, inside his head, as clearly as if he'd said it aloud.

"Oh, shit," it says. "You're a goner, buddy."

Yes, he is already gone. Simon is done for.

It is comedy. It is tragedy. It is two people who just met fucking each other on a couch like it is the most important thing that has ever happened to them—and who knows if it even did.

THE TYPEWRITER

SHE AWAKENS to a "click—clickclick-click—clickclickclick" coming from her living room.

She has a moment, between sleep and awake, when she thinks she is back in her childhood home that was haunted by a typewriting ghost. It was her great-aunt who left boxes of unpublished and unread plays, who typed into the wee hours of the morning past the grave.

But Sarah is not in her childhood home. She is in her apartment. She is naked and her head is throbbing. She pulls herself out of her bed, careful not to kick off Sir Fatts and Sargeant Tubbs who don't bother to open their eyes to watch her stumble toward the sound.

The man sits, naked in a lotus position, crunched over her old electric typewriter, a cigarette in his mouth. He has lit her Jesus, Mary and Santa prayer candles—they flicker around him and the cherry on the cigarette moves and hovers like a firefly.

She stands behind him in the shadows, staring as his fingers move across the keyboard, listening to the percussive music of the clicks with the 'ding' like a chorus in a refrain.

"Hey, there," she says, as he pulls a page from the roller.

He glances over his shoulder at her, smiling. "I stole a cigarette. I hope you don't mind."

"I have cigarettes?"

"Yeah—you hadn't opened them yet and I am just cruising on them. I'll buy you another pack."

"I didn't know I had cigarettes," she says as he puts another piece of paper through the roller. "I see you found the typewriter."

"Tripped on it, more like," he says. "I hope you don't mind. I just haven't used one of these, well, since I was a kid. Thought I'd give it a ride. You were out cold. You snore like a champ."

She feels defensive, vulnerable—who is he to judge her while she sleeps? "Drunk people snore."

"You're second only to two men I know—one has a deviated septum," he says, through his cigarette.

"Drunk people snore," she says, again. "What are you writing?"

He click-clicks with one hand and hands her the page he just pulled with the other. "Read," he says.

As she sits, naked on her carpet, crouched over the paper to read by candle-light she realizes too late that she really should turn on the over-head light.

This is too creepy, she thinks.

"What do you think?" he says, as she hands him the page back.

"Spooky," she says, brushing dirt and crumbs off her naked ass from the carpet.

"Well," he says, still typing, "I am a ghostwriter."

"Huh," she says, opening her fridge and letting out a comforting rectangle of light. She is looking for a beer.

"Yes," he says. "In addition to my modicum of credit under my own name, I get paid for my silent but deadly work gentrifying the tabloid slums of the autobiographical opus."

"Hm...," she responds, finding the one beer she hid from herself behind the unidentifiable rot in the Tupperware.

"Wanna know who?" he asks.

"Not really," she says, twisting off the crown of her Bud. He is probably lying. Who is this bozo she brought home/brought her home?

"I have a ghost," she says. The ghost has a talent for spooking away suitors.

The clicky clickys stop. "Really?"

She takes six long swallows, then walks slowly back into the living room where Simon is watching her with a lean and hungry look.

"Yeah," she says, laying her body down on its side in front of him in a feline pose of purveyor. "It's rather like having a roommate."

"The only good roommate is a dead roommate," he says, agreeably, pushing out his cigarette on one of her kitchen plates. He lights another cigarette (she does recognize the box: a red gold rectangle that looks like a birthday present—where did it come from? Was she drunk?) on the Jesus candle's wick, the hum of the electric typewriter playing beneath.

"Are you trying to scare me?" she asks, staring at him in the eyes with her body naked and still.

He stares back at her, still in his lotus, smoke coming from his lips. "How so?" he says.

She sits up to drink her beer. "With what you are writing. A bunch of lies with my name and 'she said.' It's like a threat, a very stupid threat."

He starts typing again. "How so?" he says, watching the letters move beneath his hands.

"Well," she says, "you wrote that I said 'don't kill me.'"

"Yes? It's romantic. Romeo and Juliet. Death makes love passionate and meaningful."

"That's just bullshit," she says, and turns on the overhead light. He puts his hand to his eyes in a squint,

"Hey...," he says.

She is suddenly embarrassed of her own nudity, and his, in the harsh environment.

"Well," she says, clutching her beer like it's a weapon, "go away, now!"

"Sarah." He stands, holding out his cigarette so the smoke won't go into her face. He wears a mask of bemused condescension, moving his naked body toward hers. "You're trying to scare me."

"I don't know what you're talking about," she says, trying not to look in his eyes, trying to get to the bottom of her beer.

"You said you had a ghost."

"Well, I do."

"Well, weren't you trying to scare me, though? Telling me? Thinking your ghost was your watch-dog or something and you could sic it on me?"

"Her. Not it." She finishes the beer.

"That's right." He drops the cigarette butt in the bottle, the whole movement carefully choreographed to seem careless. "You have a ghost, and I write ghost stories. If I scare you, you scare me, and we both move in a little closer for comfort."

He moves in a little closer for comfort, smelling like cigarettes and her sweat and her sex and the typewriter is still humming. The overhead light is too medical, too clinical and Simon reaches a hand behind her to kill it.

Candles for wakes, birthdays and lovers.

He is gone before it is light the next morning. He leaves the typewriter in the center of the room, and the plate he used as an ashtray. The Santa Claus candle has melted to a mushroom, but Jesus and Mary, encased as they are in a prayer of glass, are still intact. He left the typewriter running but he took the pages. He left no phone number, no card, no note. She turns off the typewriter, like it's its fault.

She has the impulse to open the hood of the typewriter and remove the ribbon. It would be there — every letter — every word. It would be like looking into his head. Or his heart. Or just her stupid typewriter's innards.

The radio turns on in the other room. "Good morning," she says to her ghost. No, it is not the ghost, after all, just the clock-alarm. She set it, she remembers, because she has to go to work.

"Right," she says. "No ghost, just me."

GOOD OLD BOYS DO LUNCH

ANOTHER DAY, ANOTHER DOLLAR. Your life is work, my friend. And all work and no play makes anyone go psychotic.

You decide, in a burst of Good Young Boy, Good-Natured, Good Old Days' tribute, to invite Simon to lunch. You do have the ulterior motive of asking him about Sarah. You haven't seen her since the meeting and you are wondering... well, what happened? Are you ever gonna get lucky with that cute little hippie slut? Is Simon currently wetting his whistle with her? Maybe you can chum on, tag team like the frat days?

You make your way through the new wing they are adding to the building, through the double doors to the opposite side of the Research Center, where Simon sits, isolated in an office much smaller than yours. The door is shut and Simon has his head on his desk and his eyes closed.

You knock, opening the door. Simon snaps his head up to attention. He is sweating profusely despite the fact that they keep this place crypt-cold and you usually wear a sweater inside. He stares at you, like your interrupting his sleep was grounds for your beheading.

You give him your friendly puppy face and voice:

"Hey, Simon. I was wondering if you would like to go to lunch?"

"I don't think so," he says, wiping some drool from the side of his mouth.

"Okay," you say. "Maybe next time." You start to walk away.

He calls after you. "Dick!" he shouts.

You turn around. "Richard," you say with a calm half-smile. "Or Rich, please."

"You buying?"

"Sure," you say. "I'll buy."

You settle on a coffee shop with a deli and patio seating, which you choose because Simon insists that he smoke while he eats.

He orders two huge sandwiches, a latte and a piece of chocolate cake which he devours like he hasn't eaten in quite some time. He smokes like he's eating the cigarettes.

He doesn't talk to you at all. Doesn't even look at you. He makes loud smacking noises as he eats and blows smoke in your face. He disgusts you, or he would, if he weren't so—charismatic, you suppose is the word.

Cinderella, the story goes, was still beautiful covered in rags and soot. Simon, for all his poor manners and nasty habits, is still somehow charming and even though he won't condescend to look you in the eye, you are still proud to be in his company.

"How did you get the limp, if you don't mind my asking?" you query.

"I do mind your asking," he says. He looks at you so fiercely that you end up looking down.

"Sorry, I don't mean to bring up a sore subject."

"Then don't."

"Sorry."

He wolfs the first sandwich and starts on the second.

"How do you like working at Brighton?" you ask.

"I fucking love it. It's a fucking dream," he says.

You think of a great deal of subjects to bring up, but they all seem as lame as your lunch date. You settle for just watching him eat.

You don't say anything.
You pay the tab and walk back to the office
feeling like a grade A sucker. Which you are.
(I mean it as a compliment).

—OR—

You decide because you are paying for
lunch, after all, to have some balls
and at least find out what's up with
him and the assistant.

You got some cajones. You adjust them to make sure as he continues messily masticating. You take a deep breath and prepare, like jumping off a diving board. Then you give it to him, the line you've been rehearsing for a few hours:

"So, do you know that cute assistant, Sarah?"

You expected more of the same shrugs, even if he was fucking her.

Never in your wildest dreams would he have done what he is

doing, which is letting his jaw drop—mouth full of barely chewed sandwich, the cherry of his cigarette falling off onto his plate.

"What?" he manages.

You clear your throat. "Well, I just—um—yeah, she's nice. She said she knew you and so I—"

He throws himself over the table and grabs you by the collar.

"Are you fucking with me?" he says, his face some unrecognizable mixture of glee and anger, like he's just been waiting for some excuse—any excuse—to hit you square in the face.

Then, he drops and pulls himself back. He stands up and starts to pace around the table.

You are in utter shock, barely moving. The other patrons of the deli have noticed, but no one is doing anything. You aren't sure what to do. He just attacked you! And for what? He can't read your mind! He doesn't know what you've been thinking about her. He doesn't know that she straight up e-propositioned you. And where is she? What kind of jealous fuck is he? Does he have her locked up somewhere? Did he kill her?

This is how killers act, you tell yourself, thinking of all your experiences with killers (which is made up entirely of television shows).

He is making himself sit down now.

He is starting another cigarette. He is looking at you with a look that is so pointed, so fierce, and yet there is a smile at the edge of his lips.

"Dick," he says.

You don't, for once, correct him with your preferred shortening of your name.

"Please," he continues, inhaling. "Tell me everything you know about 'that cute assistant Sarah.'"

"Uh…" You are completely unsure of what you could possibly say to make you seem innocent. "Uh, I just, uh, talk to her sometimes."

"Do you?" says Simon, exhaling.

"Yeah," you say. God, you are fucking terrified. Simon is giving you the creeps. Your skin is fucking crawling right now, the way he is looking at you.

"I am sorry if my reaction was—shocking," Simon says, his smile growing. "I am just very interested in Sarah. She is, in fact, the reason I am here."

"You don't say," you say. Did I mention that you say very stupid things sometimes?

"I do," says Simon.

"Well, uh, yeah. She did say that, uh, you were her 'boyfriend'." You want him to know you aren't moving in on his girl. You want him to know you were not planning to tap that ass. Not for a second. Nope.

Simon is choking. Then stops, tears gathering in his eyes from the cough. He drinks some water. He puts out his cigarette. His eyes are red and he is still holding in half-coughs. When he can talk again, he says, "You don't say."

You don't understand, but you know that this is very, very serious.

"I do," you say, like you just got married.

Simon nods his head. Tears just keep squeezing out of his eyes.

A SAD BIRTHDAY CAKE

TODAY IS SARAH'S BIRTHDAY. She is turning 27. Much is made of this age by the dead celebrity obsessed, which she is. She isn't really sure of the statistics and there is probably a logical explanation for it, which she would refuse to believe.

She usually believes in the least logical explanation because it is more interesting that way, to her.

Why not?

Well, here's why not: Here it is, her birthday, and she's spooked.

She wakes up in the morning, sure the ghost in her apartment is singing "You say it's your birthday. It's my birthday, too yeah!" But then it is only the radio alarm, which is just as strange—that this song would be on at the exact moment when her alarm went off on her birthday. She finds it ominous. More so than if it were another ghost experience.

She turns off the alarm, unsure whether to thank or curse The

Universe for remembering her birthday. She has told none of her friends about this day.

She might have, had she not seen Janis Joplin last weekend in the mirror when she were tripping and had "Janis" not told her that the two of them were "one and the same" (Dead at 27).

She might have been all right with that if she had not dreamt, two nights ago, that Kurt Cobain was wearing her sweater and ran at her like an eighteen-wheeler with no brakes. (Dead at 27).

Then, to top it all off, the phone rang last night at exactly 12:01 AM and a nasally voice said, "Sarah?"

"Yes?" she answered.

There was nothing but heavy breathing.

"Who's this?" she asked.

"This is your Daddy," he said.

She laughed, thinking it could be one of her friends, trying to be funny. "Okay, 'Daddy,'" she said.

The voice went deep. "I'm coming upstairs to fuck you."

She slammed the phone into the receiver, then stood there, staring at it and shaking.

Then she remembered what her psychic friend said. "If you're afraid of the dark, turn on the lights! Fear cannot exist in the light! Confront it—you are a child of God and nothing can harm you!"

It is precisely the wisdom of the busty doomed broad in all the horror movies—sure, go see what's making that noise in the base-ment. Thus arming herself with a kitchen knife she stormed down the apartment steps to see if her so-called 'Daddy' was down there.

There was nothing at all down there but the dark early moments of her birthday, and she had made it to minute three alive.

She managed to fall asleep after unplugging the phone (why not?) and taking three healthy shots of whiskey (it's her birthday, after all) and singing herself to sleep with Cole Porter songs. (*All through the Night* is like a night-light in her vocal cords).

Now, awake and still alive, she eats exactly 27 jellybeans for breakfast with a huge cup of coffee. Yum!

After her jellybean breakfast, she goes to her place of sucker employment, Brighton Research Center. Her job pretty much sucks: data entry, customer service, assisting upper-management; but her co-workers are very pleasant people to spend time with and there is always a steady stream of temps who keep it interesting.

They knew it was her birthday at work because they have her paperwork. Her department assembles a small gathering in the kitchen over a supermarket cake with "Sarah" in blue cursive letters and 28 candles (one for good luck). She closes her eyes and makes a wish, a very simple wish, which can be told because it doesn't come true.

She wishes to make it to 28.

Around four o'clock she is looking at a 57 page printout of customer names and the letters start swirling together like they are going down a drain. It is a common trick of her eyes that means it is time to look at something else. She gets up to dump her half-finished tepid coffee and replace it. In the Company Kitchen, her cake sits on the table, half of her name eaten, the other half looking sad, waiting for some destination.

The phrase "a sad birthday cake" occurs to her, and it seems like such a lovely, appropriate phrase she is shocked to be the first person who thought of it. And then tears come to her eyes; she doesn't know why, but something about that cake makes her so sad.

JOY IN THE MORNING

"JOY, THERE WILL BE JOY, JOY, JOY! There'll be joy in the morning!" She is singing her part, soprano. She is singing *Joy in the Morning* even though it is late in the afternoon.

She is outside, in the parking lot. The light reflects strange and bright flashes.

She wishes she had sunglasses.

The parking lot is full of cars but no people. A bird flies overhead, and a bit of dandelion fluff soars in the air above her head. She thinks of the desert where she found herself, where she still is, in a way, dancing in the darkness, dancing in the light, dancing and singing and screaming to the beat surrounded by people who are of the same purpose. It is time to go home.

She continues to sing, rather absently, thinking about a tree, a wishing tree. It is a tree in her mind, made of light with long weeping and growing branches. Each wish that she makes becomes a seed of a flower or fruit, and she imagines herself beneath that tree now, wishing birthday wishes.

The dandelion fluff hovers above her. She could grab it from the air, blow it apart with her breath and make another wish. Candles, dandelions, coins in a well, shooting stars—so many things to wish on. A breath of wind takes it apart and away.

She loses her orientation, following the pieces upward into the air and she can't remember why she came out here in the first place. Maybe she is feeling tired. Isn't it still her birthday?

A delicious feeling, sparkling inside of her says that something is going to happen—something she wants to happen, tonight. Something will change—she is that dandelion fluff and the breeze will wish her apart.

Where is it—that thing that will happen?

Maybe she will just go straight home, she is already in the parking lot. But what is she thinking? She should let the boys and girls from work buy her a birthday drink at the bar down the block from here. Who is she to turn down a birthday drink?

The dandelion pieces have scattered away and she feels herself hovering, whole, static in the presence of a confusing wind.

Does she decide that she will see all these bozos tomorrow anyway (besides who needs to hear another 'Happy Birthday' on the Birthday she's to forget?)

—OR—

Does she decide to grace the guys from work with her glorious presence and get her drink on?

BIRTHDAY PRESENT

SHE BIDS ADIEU TO THE BOYS at work, and takes their protestations like flowers showered on a beauty queen.

Her drive home blends into every other drive home from work, so that she has trouble distinguishing it. As she steps down onto the street, she finds herself wandering to her corner store, telling herself she wants to buy something, something for her birthday, a present.

She spends quite a while wandering the aisles, like she is stoned, considering each item, touching the outside packaging, trying to listen. It is a pink soda in a clear bottle that she selects, two, one in each hand. Then she gets lost in a cheap sunglasses display and places huge dark shades on her face and looks into the rectangular mirror. The reflection gives her a dizzying sense of déjà vu.

She makes her way to the counter and the man working, whom she does not recognize, smiles at her. He says something in a thick accent like "You want your smokes?"

"Excuse me?" she says, smiling back. She doesn't smoke.

He places a red and gold plastic wrapped square in front of her. He looks into the glasses at himself reflected.

His face quivers and then falls like a sad cake — like a sad birthday cake. "I thought... You are her?" he stammers, then looks right past her to the next customer, as if she weren't there at all.

She feels she is floating up far and fast and she puts her fingers around the package to steady herself and walks out. As she walks down her block, she realizes she has not paid for the sunglasses, the soda or the cigarettes.

She stops and looks both ways, deciding whether to go back now and pay, or wait until later. She decides on later.

L.A. is fading to gray; with the sunglasses, it looks like midnight. An old man in a black hat with black suspenders stops his stooped walk to regard her, frankly, with watery blue eyes. She hastens past him, afraid of his gaze, around the back way to her apartment, through the parking lot.

A parking attendant waits there, a cigarette hanging from his lips as she walks past. "Sarah," he cries after her. He is, in fact, crying.

She does not know him, but no matter, she is friendly to many people she doesn't remember. She is friendly to everyone. "Hi, Earl," she says, reading the stitching on his front pocket. Everything feels like a dream, rather pleasant in fact, and she wants to comfort him, somehow.

"Would you like a soda?" she asks. She hands him a clear cold bottle filled with the pink liquid.

He gazes into it like it is magic. She smiles and turns away.

"Is your soul at rest?" he asks.

It's a bizarre question but she knows the answer, as if this is a play she's been rehearsing. "I'm just visiting," she says.

As she walks up the back staircase he calls out again.

"Sarah!" he calls. "You don't have to stay put! Come back anytime! Come back anytime!"

She is in her hallway, the lights flicker on and then off. It isn't quite dark yet. She stands in front of her door, trying to find her breath, trying to piece together exactly what is going on.

She opens her door. Inside her apartment, hippie-purple curtains let in the last of a magical light. Inside, two red finches and two yellow canaries jump about, chirping something comical. Inside, a green parrot bids her something close to an English greeting.

She has left the radio on. "What's going on?" asks Marvin Gaye.

Happiness and home spill out and over her. There's no place like home, after all, and she joins into the choir -soprano.

She throws the sunglasses off her face with a cavalier gesture and a long held note. She opens her soda and drinks and drinks until it is gone. The soda is magic; she marvels, Earl was right. She feels like dancing in every direction, laughing and soaring through space. She feels that she could start tripping, right now, this very moment—tripping through time and space and go all sorts of places.

A voice inside her, she calls it her Inner Wet Blanket, warns her against such trips. 'Not today,' it says. 'Not right now.' It is her birthday, and she knows she would go some place groovy, but the Inner Wet Blanket knows a thing or two about putting out fires and she is trying to play it safe.

'Why?' She asks her IWB.

'You know why.' IWB responds.

'What else am I going to do?' she asks.

*Well, she could smoke cigarettes, get drunk
and take a nice, hot bath.*

—OR—

*Fuck it, trip out—the carpet is already starting to
get all smooshy beneath her feet and she only has to
say the word to be whisked through time and space...*

THE WORD, SAID

SHE SAYS THE WORD AND IS GONE. She has the giggles; she often gets the giggles during time travel. She is not scared at all because she has done this countless times before and get this: *never* while she was on drugs! See, she was born with a special gift (or curse, depending on which seat she is sitting in). Ever since she can remember she's been able to visit different dimensions (try the second for a good laugh; the ninth when you don't have anything you need to do for a few days afterwards), different galaxies, different integers in the line of human evolution. She doesn't have much control over where she goes, but she always has some control over if she goes.

She stopped going for many years. Long story why; we'll get into it later, maybe. For now, it's her birthday, and she's going some place very special.

Yes, here she is, in a humanly inconceivably ornate opera hall.

Every seat is carved in gold, diamonds, rubies, emeralds and the cushions are red and black and gold velvet. No roof—only a dark deep night with dancing stars. In the audience is everyone she has ever met or will meet mixed in with about 10,000 people she doesn't know and will not meet... this time around, anyway. Everyone is dressed outrageously, but strictly to the nines.

Her Grandpa, for example, is wearing a pink toupee to match his pink silk trousers and is sitting in the box seat with his hero, Franklin D. Roosevelt. F.D.R. looks absolutely smashing in purple tuxedo made entirely of grapes (they do not crush in the sitting down, so perhaps they are magic grapes).

Jesus Christ Himself is MC-ing this show, wearing his glowing sacred heart with a special neon-flicker. She is backstage, eating red brandied pears with Chuck Berry (who wears a suit of living, swimming goldfish, which she cannot stop raving about) and Julius Caesar (who knew he sang? Oration, she supposes, is not far from opera).

Kurt Cobain, bless him, is out on-stage now singing a lovely Carmina Burena with an orchestra of monks in monkey suits (well, actually, more gorilla suits) backing him up. Kurt is dressed like an orangutan. It is moving, funny, touching, and the audience loves it and stands in ovation.

Now it is her turn. What will she sing? Well, what is she wearing? A long gown made of pure white mist. Of course, it's her favorite— *"Misty."* She opens her mouth and her voice soars like angels, hurdling through galaxies but resonating through the opera hall, beautifully, perfectly, "Walk my way... and a thousand violins begin to play..."

She sings the whole song, in real earth time, in real earth tones, and when she is finished, she bows as the audience stands in ovation.

She bows so deeply into the mist of her own gown that she loses herself in it and the applause becomes fainter and fainter in the fog as she falls straight into herself.

THE MAN IN THE MAGIC BOX

SHE DOESN'T HAVE CABLE, but she feels like some good commercials might bring her back to harsh reality. Sarah has another cigarette. God, for a non-smoker, she is an amazingly fast learner. Or maybe she's been a chain-smoker for years and forgot.

L.A. local news is on. "The horror, the horror" calms her. She understands the carnage of 'stars upon thars' (this is a Seuss reference, natch), she comprehends who was seen where, wearing what and with whom, and she smokes and talks back to her glass teat and feels rooted in reality—until she sees him.

Him. On her Channel 9 Late Breaking news—the man who she has, has not, can't remember if she's met. Did she meet him at a bar? At a Cake-Walk? Did they fuck? Was he just here last night or is he just here tonight—talking to her, directly to her, from the magic box?

She is all wet and drunk. She just finished a cigarette. She could have another, and she will—after she touches herself watching the man whose eyes are ever so perceptibly different colors, with the most perfect pink mouth and gorgeous mocha skin, explain it all to her in lucid prose.

And once he has finished doing his commentary and she finishes doing herself, she will have another cigarette, two more shots, and stare down at the typewriter in the middle of her living room floor. She should put it back in the closet. It seems to have an agenda of its own that she isn't sure she likes.

She has a vision of Simon Would, hunched over it—naked, smoking—and can't remember if that really happened, is going to happen, or never happened.

She should really go to bed.

She drops her towel over the typewriter and stumble, dance, stumbles to her bedroom.

On the way there, she hears the rush of the bathtub faucet. It is always in one of various stages of leaking, and now it is as if she never turned it off. She twists the faucet as hard as she can. Now it is just a drip, drip, drip. It's lucky she pulled the plug when she got out of the tub, or the whole place would be flooded.

She turns to see a tall shadow in the doorway to the bathroom. She screams and a hand covers her mouth.

"Shhh...," he says, moving his hand and holding her in an embrace. "The door was open. I'm sorry I scared you."

"I just... I just saw you on tv..."

"Did you like it?" he asks, his hands sticking to the places still wet on her body.

"How did you get here so fast?"

"It's not live, silly. We tape on Saturdays. You...I cannot stop thinking about you... Sarah... I..."

"Have we met?" she mumbles. "Have we been formally introduced? I can't remember—something happened when I stepped into the bath tonight and... I can't remember anything... it's all..." and she can't ask anymore questions because she is drowning in her own gasping moans as she finds herself on the bathroom floor getting her brains fucked out—further removing the possibility of her remembering shit.

Simon goes out as he came in, a shadow, leaving her wondering if he were really there at all, or just some randy ghost, some astral projection of the real Simon Would, who does exist, who she sees the next day online. He has even posed for GQ.

He sure as shit exists enough to have stolen her typewriter.

When she leaves for work the next morning, the towel in her living room lacks the hard thing beneath it, like an ashamed, discarded condom. It could not protect her property, after all.

"That thieving asshole!" she screams. And she has no way of getting in touch with him, no way of seeking retribution for her electric word-processing artifact.

He could afford to buy his own goddamned typewriter but would rather steal from her, an assistant to three middle-management shit-heads, barely a step above a temp, who can barely make rent. It makes her sick. That's why her stomach is all a-flutter butterflying and her heart is thumping like she's dying. She feels hot like she's got a fever and starts laughing as she's crying. Oh—and seems to be rhyming.

This is more serious than she thought.

"Oh shit," she says, realizing she is, in fact, in love with him.

And that no matter how drunk she was, there was no way she left the front door open.

How the hell did he get in?

FREE SPIRITS

SARAH DECIDES TO GRACE THE SUITS with her glory. Who is she
to turn down free drinks and the company of Company Men? It's
her birthday, after all. Time to get her drink on.

After three shots called "blowjobs" (she's not sure what they
are, but they are covered in whipped cream and she's not supposed
to use her hands drinking them) and two whiskey sodas, she is suf-
ficiently toasted enough to get up and shake her groove thing to
whatever shit the boys put on the juke-box.

She feels she is being watched, which of course she is. By the
Company Men, by the Random Men, and someone else.

She finds herself drawn to him, as if on a string. God, could it
be? In this place—their little corporate watering hole and he finds
his way here—tonight? Could it really be him?

"I'm sorry," she says, approaching him with her best 'I'm a cute
girl and I'm a little tipsy' look on her face. "You look so familiar."

He is beautiful, dazzling—so much more so in person. Her vision is slightly blurred, though, and she is unsure if it really is him.

"Yes," he agrees. "You look familiar to me, too." His voice is thrilling.

She suddenly has the spins. No. It's not him. It can't be. Simon is a guy from the Other Side of the camera lens, who exists in a world of News and Media. He can't exist in the same space as she does. She is a wannabe. An aspiring. A "will never make it." She is doomed.

"Are you okay?"

"Oh yes." She stands up, making a show of smoothing herself. The boys from work are watching her with vulture eyes. Fuck 'em. It's her birthday after all. And this man, Simon or some dude who looks close enough when she's drunk, is here. She can't blow it. This could be her big chance.

"I just... I'm drunk."

She wants it to be him. She doesn't want to know if it's not.

"Do you want me to take you home?" he asks.

"Yes, more than anything," she says, and kisses him, full on the lips.

He receives the kiss, half-embarrassed, but not about to turn it down. His lips are soft and electric. He looks her in the eyes, making her see him straight. He has a half-smile on the surface of his eyes and something deeper and dangerous beneath them. Oh yes, he can do her some harm. And that's what she wants. He leads her outside. She struggles to stay upright, like a half-deflated balloon on his wrist.

She sings *"Misty"* with her perfect soprano voice. His eyes start to mist and he holds her for a moment as she sways, singing.

"You have the voice of an angel," he says. "Dear God, you are beautiful."

She always knew he would find her. She sighs his name like a prayer.

"You are a strange girl," he says.

"Strange," she says, "but lucky."

AN E-BOMB

YOU WALK IN FROM YOUR ODD LUNCH DATE with Simon, feeling…
well… a cocktail of emotions. Your head is spinning. What is the
deal with these two? After nearly strangling you, he tells you that
she is the reason he's here; and she obviously thinks he's hot (which
despite his homeless chic look you are starting to come around on)
so why can't they be together? Why is she propositioning you? Was
that some sort of mistake or a way to play mind-games with Simon?

You walk by Sarah's cubicle on your way to the men's room
(it isn't really on the way). Her cubicle is still empty. Maybe they
have moved her to a different location? That happens from time to
time-—maybe you will ask the receptionist.

You hit the men's room, pulling out your sleepy number one
who has been decidedly unlucky as of late. On your way out, you
stare at your face in the mirror—there you are, you handsome corporate tool, you. The world is your oyster. (Hey, that's why you're so

horny! Ah—you make yourself laugh.)

You return to your office by way of Sarah's empty cubicle, only—check it out—she is there... sorta. She sits motionless, staring off into her computer screen saver that is the old school galaxy and stars moving down like a tunnel.

"Sarah," you say. "Hey, where you been?"

She turns to look at you. Her face is paler than blank white copy paper.

"I didn't mean to send you that e-mail," she says softly.

Assuming she means the "get lucky" one... what the fuck? Maybe she meant to send it to Simon. Still, you feel your stomach drop with disappointment. You try to pass it off like "it's cool." Even saying, "Oh, it's cool. I figured, with Simon and all."

"Simon?" she asks.

"Yeah, I mean, your 'boyfriend.'"

"Oh my God, help me," she says suddenly with a gasp like she is choking.

Is she choking? "Are you choking?" you ask.

She shakes her head, but she is crying. You are looking around. She is causing a scene! Who else is seeing this? Over there, Lewis is looking at you strangely.

Fuck.

"I didn't mean to. I didn't mean to," she says, tears streaming down her face.

"It's okay," you say, just wanting her to shut up. "Are you feeling sick? Do you want to go home?"

She looks into the screen-saver again, nodding.

"Please," she says. "Don't say anything."

You put your hand on her shoulder.

She is so cold, a gust of freezing air seals your bones.

"Go home, now, Sarah," you say, walking away from her, feeling your own head spinning now, feeling like whatever it was, you shouldn't have touched her because now you caught it.

You should go home.

THE MEN IN SUITS

SARAH HAS BEEN STARED DOWN by her share in her day, but she's previously done a good job of steering clear of them despite her corporate dalliances. Now, however, she is struggling to maintain a brave face and proper attendance in her corporate life. She finds herself getting ill frequently and nastily. First, it was the stomach flu that left her shitting and vomiting for two days. Then there were the severe chest pains, which she suffered gladly on the clock. A ringing in her ears turned into a sharp shooting pain that landed her at the doctor's office and then a case of acute tonsillitis that rendered her literally speechless.

This was all within one month.

There is something going on at the workplace that is making her sick, but it is difficult to pinpoint if it's just the general work malaise, the incomparable, insufferable boredom, or if it's them, The Men is Suits, closing in on her at last. She starts becoming unfriendly in her own small way, unable to offer smiles or "how are you?" to her co-workers. She finds herself terrified to leave her chair lest she walk away and find herself humanly incapable of being coaxed back.

She is afraid she will shirk her earthly responsibility. She is afraid that she could and would, in fact, do something desperate.

But the time is not yet, not now. But now—or then—depending on her perspective, she will have to live with the terrible truth that man lives by the sweat of his brow and woman by inexorable pain in labor.

She decides, during the tonsillitis phase, that she doesn't need to sing after all. She just needs to find a nice man, like her mom said she should, a nice man to take care of her. Jesus, what year was that—when men "took care of" women? She thinks of her mother—frail, constantly working and not getting paid or credit—suffering under the laughable illusion that her father was taking care of her.

But she goes back to the illusion, because maybe it would become true for her. She lives in the city of dreams after all, and at any second, one could get lucky.

A chill goes through her. "A goose just walked over your grave" she thinks. A stupid phrase she has never used, but just read somewhere. An obviously outdated phrase—as if geese ever walked over graves these days.

Her co-worker, Tamara, peers over the cubicle wall.

"Who's the suit?" Tamara asks.

"What?" Sarah bolts upright in her chair.

"Behind you."

She turns, and there he is, in his preferred uniform of a business suit, his hair parted on the side, his eyes exposed: ice-cold and blue and painted on like Barbie's. He is looking over her shoulder like he is checking her work.

When she looks directly at him, he winks his evil eye and disappears. She turns back to see if Tamara has noticed the disappearing trick, but she has moved on.

Sarah jumps up from her chair and runs the course of the cubicle walls, running after Tamara like a crazed rodent in a maze.

Tamara is walking to the kitchen.

She grabs her. "What did you mean, 'who's the suit'?" Sarah demands.

"The guy behind you. Jeez, chill, Sarah."

"There was no one behind me."

Tamara rolls her eyes. "Yes, there was. Who is it? Your new boyfriend?"

Sarah feels faint, weak, sick. Something is pressing in on her mind. Bright white spot flashes. A migraine.

"Hey, are you okay?" asks Tamara. "Maybe you should go home."

War, war and more war on the horizon. Executives of businesses found dead in their cars of supposed self-inflicted gunshot wounds; 1/3 of a continent wiped out by messy love; grotesque figurines decorating discriminating homes making deals with the devil, no batteries needed; mass hysteria for mass destruction; an eye for an eye making the whole world blind; madness and infinite methods to it. White flashing light into her third-eye chakra. The End-Times approaching and what will she sing?

"Suicide is painless, it brings on many changes, and I can take or leave it if I please." Take out the lyrics and you have a popular TV theme song, but no laugh-track in the operating room. She wishes she would faint. God, make it stop now.

Tamara has taken her hand. It is so warm, so kind, and Sarah finds herself enveloping in her embrace. She smells her hair gel, her perfume, her lotion. Her blouse is gold and she is warm, alive, not one of them. They won't hurt Tamara will they? She will be okay, somehow, right?

"Honey, go home," says Tamara.

"Please," Sarah says, knowing she is not making sense, "don't tell anyone you saw me here."

SNIPE HUNT

LEWIS IS WATCHING YOU WALK from Sarah's cubicle. He gives you a suspicious sort of look.

"What?" you say.

"Who you talking to?" Lewis says.

"Lewis, I told Sarah to go home. She's sick."

"Sarah?"

"Yeah, Sarah."

"Man, there are no Sarahs who work here," he says.

You sigh. "Sarah While, the assistant to the assistant to the boss — cute — yeah. She works right over there, go introduce yourself and get to know the help —"

Lewis grabs your shoulder and whispers, his eyes all kooky-crazy intense like a rabid horse or something.

"You better not talk like that," he says.

"Like what?" you say.

Lewis is pissed. "I don't know where you got the idea that this is funny."

You are getting angry now. What is his fucking problem? He thinks you don't have the right to send Sarah home? He probably knows you are about to get promoted, that you are going to be his boss. So what if he's been here five years longer? You have the MBA and them's the breaks.

"Look," you say. "What is the problem? Level with me, man." The 'man' sounds forced and retarded coming from your mouth, which is maybe why Lewis looks like he might throw up.

He drops his voice, even though he was barely whispering.

"Man," Lewis says, "Sarah's been dead for a year now."

What?! Do you believe him?

How can you?

Because if *she's* a ghost, then fuck, maybe *all* these people are ghosts, too. Just as likely.

You have a splitting head-ache. Whatever sort of practical joke this is—you start going through the list of the ones that have been played on you. There was the snipe hunt when you were a kid... there was that time when they said there was a ghost in the frat house. Man, they had all fucking laughed at you when you screamed... it was just stupid Cameron in a sheet. That's this—they're pulling something on you. You feel it. They want you out. They want you to fuck up. They are all outside chuckling and then you are going to have to make a big "*oh!* Ha ha! You guys really fooled the dumb jock from Kansas!'

You're so over this bullshit.

You go back to your office and close the door and open your e-mail.

Shit. There's another one.

to: ricjimmy@brigtonbeach.com
from: sarawillie@brightonbeach.com
Subject: Happily Ever After
Date: 12/13/01

Message:

Can you help me?

There is something going on here, have you noticed?

It's not just that they are paging me over the loud-speaker. It's not just the new secretary or the new security guard but that they are knocking out walls for expansion and have you smelled what's coming from the drain in the bathroom?

Maybe it's just the ladies room, but the maintenance guy is constantly pouring something down there to keep it under control. I know, I know — shouldn't a bathroom smell like shit? Yes, but this is more serious than shit, shit — it wafts up the drain like someone stuck a Project Manager down there three months ago with a pen in his throat.

Seriously. I know, I know — what are you going to do — take time out of your busy schedule to deal with death?

Not in this corporation. People walk around in their various stages of cancer: acquiring, battling, remitting, submitting; each with their own death toll lists. A public company knows a lot of dead.

Here in California, though, we don't think too much about too much. When I take a nap in my car at lunch, I catch these moments of beauty in an all-encompassing pleasant forgetfulness, a salve in a perfect gem of feeling, or a cotton swab of a thought. If dying could be just like falling asleep, no one would ever feel bad. Esp. about the babies dying. Babies are supposed to sleep.

But people don't think it's really like sleeping. Not if they gots any smarts. Cause you ain't sleeping, sweetie.

Except for all those beautiful dead princesses in fairy tales — in glass coffins at the heart of the forest, behind thick walls of thorns near a loom...where death is not death, and sleep is not sleep, and beauty and goodness hold hands and kiss and true love happens between royalty and the commoner when the right midget spins straw.

Do you think that might happen to me? Do you think this administrative assistant might land the President of the corporation if I play my cards right? After a couple of drinks his eyes get that hungry look, like he doesn't just want strippers, but that girl who he is not supposed to harass, who is too smart to risk it with. But HE isn't too smart. That's the whole thing.

Don't ask him about it, unless you want to be the one under the drain in the ladies room looking up at skirts while you slowly die of a pen in the trachea.

Well, I gots to get back to the job... slogging minutes into hours into days into some sort of penance for dreaming too hard for too long...

There is a message for you. When Simon Would offers you a happy ending, take it. Take it and run with it. At least he will end up in a better place then. And you, too.

Who are you? Do I know you? Can you help me? Seriously. Check out the new wing.

And seriously, someone is dead beneath the drain in the ladies bathroom. Is anybody missing? Is it you?

Seriously.

XOXOXOXOXOXOXOXOX

SW

Now you are furious. What is this? Some sort of sabotage of the spooky? She's in cahoots with Lewis and Tamara and probably Simon as well, trying to get you to slip up because they know, as you know, that you are about to be promoted—and shit, she's probably fucking the Boss. This is what she meant about the e-mail. She'd just sent this to you when you went over to talk to her. Didn't mean to send it? What did she mean, then? No one writes an e-mail this long they don't mean to send.

Did she already go home, or is she still wandering around? You better page her—quick—before she leaves. You know her type—she'll crumble. She'll say what's really going on and who put her up to it.

You pick up your phone and look for her name on the company roster.

It figures, you suppose, that it would not be there. In fact, there are no Sarahs or Saras or Casaura Sauras of any sort and you are pissed and bewildered. Was Lewis telling the truth? No, of course not. Maybe she goes by her middle name. You call the front desk.

Jocelyn, the new highly professional receptionist says, "Yes, Mr. Jamison?"

"Would you please page Sarah While and ask her to come to my office, please?"

"I'm sorry, Mr. Jamison..." she says. "I don't have an extension for Sarah While..."

"That's why I said to page her, Jocelyn." You are trying to keep from losing your temper because you are a young man and still a relatively new hire and you want to keep your reputation. You are on the verge of being on the verge of being promoted.

Over the loudspeaker, Jocelyn says in an even voice, "Sarah While, please report the Mr. Jamison's office. Sarah While, please report to Mr. Jamison's office immediately."

Good job, Joceyln. Exactly. You need to print this e-mail as evidence. You may need to make a formal complaint, but now you just leave it, like a striking rectangle of evidence, on your screen. You lean back in your chair and lace your hands behind your head.

You make your face as even as possible. You can be cool about things. You may still want to fuck her, after all. Your fingers start to tingle behind you head.

There's a knock on your door. "Come in," you say, putting the power in your pose.

Simon Would stands in your doorway, his hands sort of shaking and his face very excited. "Come on," he says. "Let's take a break. Right now. Hurry."

"Uh, Simon," you say. "I actually just paged Sarah regarding an e-mail and—"

"She sent you an e-mail?"

"Yes, but—"

Simon shoves you over to look at your monitor.

"What the—?" you try to get out, but he literally has his hand in your face, his arm out—holding you back. He is surprisingly strong. He also reads very fast. Then he looks at you, letting his hand out of his face.

"Have you ever seen the movie *Terminator*, Dick?" he asks.

"Uh, yeah. It's Rich."

" 'Come with me if you want to live.' " He smiles. It is a dazzling smile and you are dazzled, even for the moment, by the promise it has of every seen and unseen movie-fantasy fulfilled.

He makes a stage whisper: "Meet me out back. Go out the back way. That's the only way there's a happy ending, that way. For you and me."

And then he scampers, runs, bolts, makes a break for it.

You aren't sure what to do.

You are about to call Jocelyn again when she shows up at your door. Her arms are crossed and she has the security guard and the Boss behind her. The Boss, your Boss, who was not a day ago shaking your hand like he wanted to fuck you, is now shaking your neck like he wants to strangle you.

"You...sick...twisted...fuck...," he says, his head red and throbbing less red and throbbing than your-about-to-pop-off head.

The security guard and Jocelyn manage to pull his arms off your neck enough for you to pull yourself away in horror.

"What?" you cry from your aching throat. "What is going on here?"

The Boss calms himself by taking some pills out of his pocket and swallowing them.

"Sorry, Jamison," he says. "I didn't mean to kill you, I just have... a nasty temper. And high blood pressure. You understand."

You find yourself nodding like you do.

Now Jocelyn steps up—cool, professional Jocelyn—to slap you across the face.

"That's for making me part of your sick joke," she says.

"What joke?" you say, face smarting.

She starts to cry. "You told me to page... Sarah While... and everybody heard, and thought it was my fault. Do you know what people have been saying to me?"

"No," you say.

You might as well come clean. Fold 'em.

"Look, Sarah sent me this very inappropriate e-mail and I wanted to speak to her about it."

The Boss grabs your neck again and shakes it, "You...sick...

twisted...fuck...," like this is the chorus to a song, and your head the percussive maraca that makes it a pop favorite.

He doesn't need to be pulled off; he is too tired and falls into your chair. He doesn't have another chorus in him.

"Let's see this e-mail," he says. You point to your computer screen. Your Boss swivels in your chair to read.

Jocelyn stands over his shoulder, eyes moving across the computer screen. The security guard just stands in the doorway and looks dumb.

"You write this, Jamison?" the Boss asks, without finishing it (you know he doesn't read that fast).

"No, sir! She sent it to me, as I said..."

"Well, that's impossible. You know why that's impossible?"

You shake your head.

"You think that's possible that he doesn't know why that's impossible?" your Boss asks Jocelyn. Of course, Lewis' joke on you is now presenting itself as not a joke at all, and suddenly you are presented with the far more terrifying prospect of being that *Sixth Sense* kid.

Double-fuck.

A WAY OUT

JOCELYN IS STUDYING YOU while answering the boss. "He's new like me. Like him." She points to the Security Guard. "We didn't know until today."

"Well, it's impossible," says the Boss, "that she sent this e-mail because she is dead, Jamison. She has been dead for a year, boy." White spittle collects in the corners of his mouth.

"A ghost," murmurs Jocelyn, "who writes e-mails from beyond the grave." Her voice lilts up like a camp counselor around a campfire.

"How did she die?" you ask the Security Guard, who of all people seems the least likely to physically harm you. The Security Guard shrugs.

"The flu. A car accident. How the fuck should we know?" says your Boss. "We aren't morbid fucks at Brighton. She died, and we kept our mouths shut. Out of respect. I suggest you do the same."

The Boss motions to Jocelyn who shakes her head at you and

exits. The Boss motions to the Security Guard who says, "Sorry fella," and then punches you in the gut and exits.

The Boss stays behind. He doesn't touch you but fixes you with both of his evil eyes. "This is a warning. We keep our mouths shut. Out of respect. I suggest you do the same." Then the evilest eye gives you a wink. Then he gives you a pat on the shoulder with a good-old boy chuckle, and exits.

You are stunned at the sudden turns: spook-seeing? E-mails beyond the grave? *Three Stooges* type physical punishment? You'd think this was a joke, if you hadn't just been choked, slapped, and socked in the gut.

Fuck.

So. You are here. Now, ask yourself, why?

"Am I here to be a corporate tool?"

If so, then you must listen to your Boss. Think about your Promotion. Keep your mouth shut. Get back to work. (Repeat until The End of Time).

Seriously, now, GET BACK TO WORK!

That is... until your boss meets you in the parking lot and puts a pen through your throat for knowing too much and puts you in a crawl-space beneath the restroom that is to be filled with concrete within the next few days.

A sad ending for you, no doubt.

— *OR* —

Think not about your promotion, just think about your guitar: You aren't

*here to be a corporate tool, you're here
to make the ladies drool, dance like a
fool, play guitar real cool, and fucking
rule rock and roll old school, right?*

That's right.

"Come with me if you want to live."

MEMORIES

SARAH SMILES AT YOU.

"It's okay," she says. "Don't be freaked out. I remember past lives the way most people remember their childhood. Snippets and things. You can make some linear sense of it, but not easily. It more comes like, 'oh, I remember that episode from three lives back.' The further back the lives are, the less I remember them. Anyway, I try not to talk about it too much. I wish I had a better gift."

"Like what?" you ask.

"Like being able to remember the future. Wouldn't that be great?"

"And much more useful" you say, thinking of the lottery.

"Yeah," she says. "I'd know which ones were poisonous," she says. "Which ones to let lie—and not lay." She laughs.

God, you are drunk. She is drunk, too. What a party!

HAPPY MOVIE ENDING

RIGHT ON, FRIEND.

You see, your Boss was so sure you were a tool, he didn't even touch your freaking computer.

Now, hit *"Print."*

You have some evidence of some something-something. You got a little hop-scotch in your step. That double strangle chorus and ominous spittle coda was just what you needed to wake the fuck up. Better than a double espresso latte to get the juices going.

You walk in a quick-fire jaunt over to the printer. You are getting strange and nasty looks from your co-workers who have been here longer than a year. That's most of them.

Friends of Sarah. Little do they know that you are her new best friend. Is she materializing braless for THEM? Is she sending them sexy cryptic e-mails from beyond the grave? You pick aforementioned sexy cryptic e-mail up from the printer, see Tamara, who is looking like she might want to start a refrain of the Boss-Shake-Spittle and Roll, but you are out the back too quickly.

Simon stands outside the double doors, smoking, waiting for you. The instant you walk through he throws down his cigarette and screams "RUN!"

He is surprisingly speedy for a gimpy chain-smoker.

You race to his car, (you assume) a green BMW covered with bird-shit and dust, and now you're barreling out of the parking lot.

"Key Card!" he screams at you.

"What?" you scream back.

"Fuck it!" He has already gone through the parking garage's key-card operated mechanical arm. The BMW spins a little, but he regains control and you continue barreling down the block.

You look over your shoulder. No one is chasing you.

Twenty minutes later, you are standing in line at LAX. Simon returns from the vending machines with two small bags of chips: Nacho Cheese and Salt 'n Vinegar.

"It's gonna be a long flight," he says, breaking into the Salt 'n Vinegar.

"I still don't see why we had to run," you start.

He motions for you to keep your voice down. "There's a lady behind you. With Pomeranians," he whispers.

"I still don't see," you whisper, "why we have to go to Bermuda."

"We don't have to go to Bermuda. We want to go to Bermuda," he says. "We need a place to lay low. I have a condo on the beach. Time-share."

"I don't see why we have to lay low. All we did that was illegal was break the... what do you call that arm-thingee?"

Simon doesn't know.

"It doesn't matter about the arm-thingee. What matters is that

Sarah is trying to tell us something."

"What do you mean, us? She appeared to me. And she sent me the e-mail."

"But she gave me the limp."

"When?"

He looks clueless and embarrassed as a battered spouse. "It was probably my fault."

"Do you think the Boss killed her and her body's beneath the drain in the ladies bathroom?" you ask, proud of your new attempt at Holmesian deduction.

Simon motions again for you to keep it down. The lady behind you covers her Pomeranians' ears.

"No," says Simon. "That's probably the Project Manager that disappeared. You replaced him. God, I want a cigarette."

"Wait—how do you know Sarah? Why did she appear to me? And how did Sarah die?"

"In Bermuda, Dick."

"Rich."

"It'll all be clear in Bermuda." Simon cracks his neck. "I think I want to go buy one of those neck pillows. You know, the ones that look like cashews? You want one? Or some cashews for that matter? I'm buying."

Thirty minutes later you are on a flight to Bermuda, eating salted cashews and looking out the window at the L.A. smog line. Simon is snoring in his neck pillow.

Thirty days later you have a regular gig playing Nirvana and Pearl Jam covers at the local bar on the beach.

Thirty weeks later, you are still spending your days drinking spirits out of coconuts, nights making music, like making love, out of nothing at all.

Simon and you have a routine dialogue. It is a duet you sing with each other each night as the sun sets. It goes like this:

You: "Simon, did you know Sarah had pictures of you on her desk at work? She didn't know you then, did she? Yet she still had all those pictures... those were you, right?"

Simon: "Yes, you are probably right, Dick; when I was too fat and non-smoking and didn't have this charming hobble. That was me, Dick, before Sarah."

You: "Rich, please."

Simon: "Yes. I was rich."

You: "How did you get the limp, again?"

Simon: "I fell. I slipped in Sarah's bathroom, then I slipped down Sarah's steps. It never mended and I never cared. I was drunk for a long, long time, Dick."

You: "Richard."

Simon: "Right. Then I remembered I was still a journalist, a goddamn investigative reporter, and I would have to find out what happened to Sarah. So I got myself hired at the last place she worked, and I snooped around."

You: "And?"

Simon: "And I found The Men in Suits were the culprits. But there's really not much you can do. You can't bring The Men in Suits to justice."

You: "Why, Simon?"

Simon: "They're demons, Dick."

You: "Richard."

Simon: "They're demons, Richard. They circle the earth doing what they are told. Tool demons, Richard."

You: "Why did they want Sarah, Simon?"

Simon: "She knew too much, Dick. She knew too much."

A pause.

You: "What did she know?"

Simon: "It's all in the book. You'll know, Dick, everything, when I finish. I'm very close, now. Very close."

You: "It's just too bad, for poor Sarah."

Simon: "It is. It sure is. It's a goddamn tragedy. Her poor ghost wandering around that company. Sitting in front of that computer. Typing e-mails. It's almost as bad as being alive and working there. Maybe worse."

You: "You'd think, dead and all, she'd be in a better place."

Simon: "You'd hope so. It's a goddamn tragedy."

A respectful pause. You both sip your drinks.

Simon: "The important thing, though, Dick—"

You: "Rich,"

Simon: "Right. Rich, Dick, Richard, buddy, lover—listen to me!"

You: "Sorry."

Simon: "The important thing, though, is that *WE'RE* in a better place."

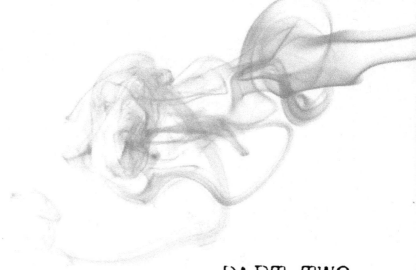

PART TWO –
THE NEWS

Wherein...

Simon buries,

burns

or brings it.

TIME TRAVEL

I WAS THIS PERSON—this other person that I can hardly recognize now as me.

Imagine, if you will, that you are stuck in a room watching a small, strange movie. The movie is in pieces, different edits, different cuts, and you put them together and watch. You feel disconnected from all the characters, but sorry for them. You feel that they have nothing to do with you, but this is all you can do, watch this movie.

You cannot leave this room or stop watching these pieces of this movie until you find a clue. You have no idea what the clue will be, but there is a key that will unlock this room you are in, and then you can leave. You can burn down the room if you like. Or just walk away. It doesn't matter.

But for now, you are stuck watching this movie. And one of the characters—the one that seems so unlike you in so many ways, the one that is the most foreign, this strange girl—well, you are told that once upon a time that girl was you.

Or not. Because actually, it could have been any of them. They are all you.

Day after day you watch them, and they are oblivious. They can't see you, they don't know that you are there. They don't feel your eyes or sense your concern or questioning. They don't know that you are trapped. They don't know that you are watching their pathetic little lives looking for a clue.

And your pity, and your detachment starts to sour.

They know nothing of you. They care nothing for you. They are gone—only preserved in this stupid piece of film that is now the instrument of your torture. You start to hate them. You start to really, truly hate them.

I'm sorry—not *you*. *You* aren't stuck at all. You aren't even here. You are just a person on the other side, there, going about your business like nothing at all, like none of us are here, suffering because of the thoughtlessness of your actions, the discontentedness of your drama, the back and forth of it all.

It is *me* I am talking about. You don't see *me* at all.

But you will. Because I promise you, when I find the key, I will find you. And you will suffer for your thoughtlessness and your refusal to see. You will pay.

I will get you where you sleep.

THE SPOOK PIECE

SIMON STRUGGLES TO MAKE MEANING of it all. Not sense, necessarily—he knows better than to try and find logic in the actions of men and women—but some sort of deeper meaning, for himself if no one else. There is something about this girl—it's as if he knew her, though of course he didn't. A romantic, tragic... he struggles to ding the appropriate adjective, he who is never at a loss for ten dings, but it defies defining.

Simon called it a Spook Piece, a fluffy filler piece designed to send shivers up the spines of the readers and make them think there is, after all, more in heaven and earth than philosophy so thank God they never studied it.

Simon wasn't into Spook Pieces, since he considered himself, and was well-considered, a legitimate journalist of the highest and rarest sort. He did occasional television reporting and commentaries that received the highest ratings since he was empirically gorgeous; but he was just as committed to his editorials and coverage of serious issues since he had incisive smarts that rivaled the most renowned of intellects on any given subject.

He was just unlucky enough to have finished a cover story for the *Times* on Anxiety and Depression and the drugs that treat or fail to treat them, and be walking to the soda machine when the Boss Man needed someone to catch.

It should have been Charlie, but Charlie was overseas doing the piece that by rights should have been Simon's. So, it was a miracle that Simon was doing the story at all. Simon didn't even usually drink soda. The Boss made up some story about how it fit right in with Simon's recent work on Anxiety and Depression and how he would find the reason this seemingly happy, pretty, well-adjusted young girl would slit her own wrists like she was carving her first turkey.

Simon reminded his Boss that legitimate papers don't write stories about suicide, and the Boss gave him that look that meant he was about to blow his wad. As far as the autopsy could tell, the death was not suicide. And the police couldn't call it homicide. It was in that other category: "Unnatural causes."

Simon had spread across his desk a copy of the police report, the coroner's report, a statement from the downstairs neighbor and two pictures: a head-shot and dead-shot. Both black and white and 8 by 10. She was arrestingly pretty in both.

In the picture where she was dead, she seemed to be floating—was floating, in fact, in a bathtub. But most people didn't float in their bathtubs, even if they were dead. Especially if they were dead—especially if they drowned. But the cause of death wasn't drowning. No water in the lungs. The cause of death: suffocation.

Two light finger-mark bruises in the center of her chest and one between her eye-brows. No fingerprints. No fingerprints any-where. Sure, the apartment had been flooded but no finger-prints on the razor she apparently used to slit two huge crosses in her wrists before she went to the tub where she didn't drown and didn't bleed to death but died of suffocation.

One could surmise she was killed—plastic bag over the head or something then her wrists slit afterward, which is why there was so little blood; her heart had already stopped beating. Someone kills her and makes it look like a suicide.

But there was no sign of a break-in, so maybe one of her friends (it's always someone you know, right?), and this "friend" is so clever that no fingerprints are left anywhere.

That's Simon's best guess. The police are fools, as per usual, to rule out homicide just because of lack of break-in evidence and fin-gerprints. What about the finger-mark bruises? Aren't those finger-prints enough?

And now Simon has his crusade. The detectives are obviously high, and it's going to take a hell of a reporter to get them to get their ass in gear and embarrass them into doing their job.

Yes, he will do his best investigative journalism and track down the story here—spooky, obviously—and he starts to get excited like maybe he just got lucky because this could be one of those big shocker spook pieces that will make him the next Capote.

He'll find the murderer—probably some unassuming looking guy with a sick mind who she was friends with... and what kind of friends did she have and what kind of girl was she? Was she a quiet girl, a girl who stayed home and quietly pursued her dreams? A girl who just wanted some guy in a White Hat to ride up and save her? Or was she a wild girl, the sort of girl who slept around and did weird kinky things?

He finds himself staring into space, thinking of strange things like parties he'd been to before he was married. He thinks about the girls who open his mail and answer his phone. Did they think of this as their day job? Probably. They're probably a gaggle of aspiring singers and actors, or used to be before they wised-up. Like this girl, the dead girl, they're doing a day job and pursuing tabloid dreams.

He finds himself tracing her initials as he starts to pull information. Her initials—the dead girl's—are his initials. Sarah While. Simon Would. If they were married, there would be no way to distinguish their towels, he thinks, smiling, picturing his monogrammed towels, his and hers, both with "SW" instead of "SW" and "LW." Where are those towels, anyway? He hasn't seen them in a while.

Monogrammed towels. What a world.

Sarah's family has been contacted; she's survived by a mother, a father (still married) and older brother. Her remains are to be cremated. He wants to tell them to wait, to wait in case there's more to find. There's more to find in that body of hers before it gets buried—clues in crevices they have forgotten to look, negatives still undeveloped in her dead eyes and if he can look into them—see what color they are—he will be able to see what she saw. And he will have the words to tell.

No, of course it doesn't matter. They can burn the body. He knows what he needs to know. He doesn't need to find the murderer for crying out loud, he just needs to find a way to tell the story so that the readers will be scared, and thank him for telling them what to fear. (Be afraid of your pretty daughter's dreams, for they may lead to her unnatural, horrible and scary end). Of course, there are no spooks. Just stories and the way to tell them.

He was accosted by the soda machine around 4:00 and by 6:30, he's churned out six paragraphs and his job here is done.

A piece of cake. As he walks to his car, whistling to himself, he keeps thinking "piece of cake" and recalls a Charity Cake-Walk he attended, where Charlie had fallen over right into a big pink cake. It was so funny he still laughs in the remembering.

Simon pushes the button to turn off the alarm on his BMW opening the lock. He sits down in the drivers seat, pulls on his seat-belt, and sniffs. He smells lilacs. He turns his head to see an envelope sitting in the passenger's seat with his name typewritten on the front.

Simon jumps, hits his head, scrambles to get out of his seatbelt and leaps from the car. He stands outside his car, talking himself down. He is the only one with keys, after all. He has a trigger-happy alarm that had not been triggered.

The parking garage is still except for a hum from the lights. Simon reaches into his car and carefully takes out the envelope. He opens the envelope and inside is a typewritten message. It says:

Dear Mr. Would,

It would mean a great deal if you would please investigate the strange so-called 'suicide' of Sarah While. Talk to Adam Heath (lives in Hollywood); Frank Tudor (Studio City) or Detective Walter Dervish (in Venice). They will have meaningful information for you. This is not 'a piece of cake'! It is a bloody mess!

Love,

An adoring fan

Simon is spooked at the cake bit. Sure, it can be nothing but a coincidence that he just happened to be thinking "piece of cake" but he still has the willies. He wants to burn the note. He wants to get out of the parking garage. He does not want to sit in his car, which now feels like the scene of a... spook out. He checks the back seat, the trunk, the glove compartment and the underbelly looking for anything at all out of the ordinary. (A bomb? A body?) Finding nothing, he has to decide whether to use his still virgin cigarette lighter to burn the note, bury it in the trash, or bring it with him (why does it give him the shivers? It's just a goddamned piece of paper in an envelope).

Does he...

Burn it?

—OR—
Bury it?

—OR—
Bring it?

BURN IT

A RATIONAL MAN WITH A RATIONAL MIND, Simon decides it is best to burn it. He turns the key in the ignition and Kurt Cobain screams, *"Am I the only one? Oh oh oh oh. Am I the only one?"*

Simon screams as well, then turns off the radio. He always turns off the music before he gets out of the car. He never listens to the radio. He doesn't think he'd even listened to music in the car this morning — hadn't he been rehearsing his commentary for taping tomorrow? Simon drives home checking his mirrors with scared, suspicious glances to himself.

What does he expect to see, the ghost of a hitch-hiker in the passenger seat? A man with an axe in the back seat? Was that a hook scraping on his roof? Someone had broken into his car somehow. So what? His fear was irrational — born of the stuff of urban legends. His gut told him that the note was from her, the dead girl, and that was flat out ridiculous. He presses in the button of the lighter.

He has to let go of the fear so he could find the logical conclusion.

The button pops. He pulls it out, and presses the note to the red-orange coil. First, it is simply a smoking cornered, side-blackening rectangle. He sits, silent, in traffic, flaming evidence in his right hand as his left hand grips the steering wheel. Finally it is just enough ash to fill his ashtray and as it smolders into obliteration, a calm comes over him. As he pulls off the 10 freeway the truth hits him with a peaceful, soporific narcotic.

He doesn't care if it is a bloody mess; it isn't *his* bloody mess. He is done. Six paragraphs placed on his Boss' desk and he has the whole weekend in front of him to play house. He has a television spot tomorrow—he is commenting on—yawn...

It wasn't the issue, it was how it was issued: the way he would hold the microphone, look into the camera, speak directly to all the people in America watching network news, and communicate that he, Simon Would, is a vigilant observer, a keen reporter, an invaluable weapon against injustice, deceit, and ignorance. He would be speaking into the one-eyed glass about the time they cremated her body.

Wait, what did that matter?

He pulls into his driveway as the motion sensor light comes to attention and greets his arrival. This is his house. This is his life. His piece of the pie. A piece of cake. It is not his bloody mess, he need not even wash his hands of it—they're already clean.

He dreams that night of the Men in Suits. He knows who they are, but he has not seen them in so many years he does not think they really exist, even as he sees them.

In his dream, they sit in his car, examining his radio, emptying his ashtray into a clear plastic bag. The ashes are better than nothing.

They will match them with her ashes.

How did he know to burn the letter? How does he know they will burn her? Oh, yes—he wrote the article. They will cremate her tomorrow at—what number was that?

They seal the plastic bag and look towards his front door—as if they can smell him seeing them. The one with the bag of ashes moves silently to the window outside his bedroom. Simon knows he must keep his eyes shut. They will see he is sleeping, not looking. If they see his eyes are open, they will know he knows they are there. They are already suspicious. How did he know to burn the letter?

The Man in the Suit lifts one white finger to the window and taps: one, two, three. He wants Simon to open his eyes. He wants Simon to see he's there. If Simon sees him, the Man can take him. Simon will not open his eyes. The Man taps again: one, two, three.

Glued shut—sewn shut—Simon thinks. Do not open. Cannot open. A pause. A trick. Last chance. Tap, tap, tap.

Lucy stirs in the bed next to him. He wants to warn her, tell her not to open her eyes, to keep perfectly still, but this is part of the trick. "Go away," he thinks. "Go away. I will not see you now."

"Go away," He hears a woman's voice, distinctly, inside his bedroom. A strange voice, sweet, high. "You cannot touch him. Go away."

She is like a holy water, cross, sunshine combo on vampires. The two Men in Suits near the car scatter and the one near the window is too close to escape unscathed.

Light hits the Man's face like a particle and a wave, burning through to the other side, so that his face is pock-marked invisible through to the other side before he can get away. She smells of lilacs in a rainstorm. She is still here in his room. If he opens his eyes now, he will see her, but she says with a smile in her voice:

"Simon says sleep."

And he is thrust immediately into a sleep too deep to dream.

Simon wakes Saturday morning and the only thing he can almost remember, staring at his coffee, is that he should have ashes in his BMW's ashtray. He had finished an article, he had received a letter. He had burned the letter in his ashtray in his car. He had a dream about The Men in Suits emptying his ashtray.

Who are the Men in Suits? He shakes his head.

"What are you shaking your head about?" asks Lucy.

"I... nothing. This story."

"Tell me about it."

Simon shakes his head again. "It's over. The story's already written."

But the ashtray, it is very important, should be full. That is proof that it was all just a dream. He burned it, after all.

He walks out to his car, half-muttering, clinging to his coffee cup.

A few ashes cling desperately, misting the corners, but the ashtray is empty, after all.

BURY IT

IF ONE IS BEREAVED, "bury" usually means something about digging a deep hole and putting the wrapper of what one has lost deep inside of it.

If one is a lawyer, a politician, or another party guilty by occupation, "bury" usually refers to a piece of evidence dropped in a deep hole and covered with something more confusing than dirt.

For Simon, it means stuffing the letter as far down into the nearest trash receptacle as his sense of hygiene allows.

He doesn't like to remove other pieces of garbage to insert his piece of garbage beneath, especially when his garbage is paper and the other garbage consists of cigarette butts, smelly food receptacles and mystery items. But ashes to ashes, trash to trash.

Simon has a sanitary hand wipe in the glove compartment of his car, so he buries the letter deep in the pile of refuse, wipes his hands clean of it, and goes about his business of Thanking God it is Friday.

He has a television appearance, an editorial commentary on Senator Whozinahsnatch's recent sex scandal, to be taped on Saturday afternoon. Simon has written many lovely sentences to be meted out in a calm, fair manner. He wears a lovely gray suit and a deep red tie. The camera "loves" Simon, so to speak, because unlike all the other reporters, he appears to lack a sharp stick rammed in his sphincter.

Also, he is "easy on the eyes" or "hot as hell" depending on who you ask.

"It is not about his sexual position, but his political position," Simon reminds the viewers.

The production assistants love him. The cameraman loves him. The news crew loves him. Simon loves himself.

Past the camera, in the back of the studio, a pretty girl wearing a flimsy dress watches him. She is a little distracting, but he's not the type to be distracted.

His work there done, Simon stands in the Green Room and finishes his coffee. The girl stands by the doorframe and continues to watch him. She looks familiar. She also looks practically naked, and he has the instinct to put his suit jacket over her.

He has to walk in her direction to leave, and as he comes closer he asks, "Do I know you?" She shakes her head, then puts a finger to her lips and motions for him to follow. She is leading him outside, where he was going anyway.

"Please," she says. "I have something terribly important to show you. Will you drive me somewhere?"

Simon figures she isn't a nut-case, or how would she have gotten inside the lot? Then again, most of the people on the lot are nut-cases. And further more, what is she wearing? Can she really be out in public wearing that? However he misgives, he continues to lead her to his car. He has the look of someone who is sleepwalking, hypnotized.

He is *Bewitched, Bothered and Bewildered*, which she is singing for him as he realizes he is driving down the 10 freeway East with a girl in a see-through dress he hasn't even really met.

They don't speak. She just sings, and he finds himself weeping at the meaning of the lyrics and the perfectly blended mixture of sweetness and sadness in her voice.

He must have been in a daze, for he drove for two and a half hours, without realizing time or space, but found his BMW traveling over roads that could barely be called roads to a rock canyon.

He stops the car as she stops singing, parking next to a green Ford Tempo with Missouri plates. The sun is starting to set, and the wind whips the girl's dress around her so it seems that she has trails of mist or smoke. She is more than naked; he feels he could see right through her. He feels that he has never seen a more beautiful creature in his life, that he would follow her to the ends of the earth without her asking, and she doesn't ask; he just follows her higher and higher up a towering rock, where a figure stands at the summit.

When Simon finally arrives to the plateau at the tip, she is already there, facing him, while the other figure, a man, faces outward. The man does not seem to see her, or notice her at all. He clutches something in his arms like a chest of treasure. Simon stands behind, catching his breath, unsure of what to do next, when the man cries, "I love you, Sarah!" and pulls the treasure in his arms apart to release a cloud into the sunset, and the girl, looking directly at Simon, steps backwards off the cliff.

Simon screams "No!" and rushes to the edge.

Dark shadows submerge the base of the rock. Without thinking, Simon starts to scale down. The man, a young man, with skin like whole milk and leaking eyes as blue as a metaphor, watches as Simon blubbers, "Help me! She fell! Help me!"

Simon slips, and drops nine feet on his ankle, which cracks, then he skates an additional ninety on the same ankle and other parts of his body to the dark base of the rock.

He can't find her. He crawls, the only pain he consciously feels is that he's lost her. He didn't know her name, didn't know what to call her, so he gives her the last name he heard: "Sarah."

That turns out to be right. He doesn't know how long he is down there, screaming and bloody, but it is still light outside when the man from the top of the cliff pulls him out of the darkness and to the flat sand.

"Sarah—the girl—she was right next to you—she fell—she's down here, somewhere." Simon says.

"Are you all right? We need to get you to a hospital, man."

"We have to find her..."

And the young man gasps. He takes Simon's bloody hand and shakes it.

"Oh my God," he says. "You're Simon Would."

He grabs bleeding, broken-boned Simon in a bear hug embrace. "You're here to help Sarah!"

A rush comes into Simon that sends him blissing like he's rolling on several hits of ecstasy. Yes. It all makes sense, now. He is Simon Would. He is here to help Sarah.

ANIMAL STYLE

SIMON AGREES THAT IT WOULD BE BEST if the young man, Brandon, drives him to the hospital. They also agree it is best for Brandon to drive Simon's car, and that a drive through In-N-Out is the most appropriate action en route.

"Are you sure? You're feeling okay?" asks Brandon, slowing down near Rancho Cucamonga at the bright yellow arrow.

"I've never felt better," says Simon, bleeding on the passenger seat. It is true.

"Can you get me a double-double? Animal style?"

They eat in the parking lot and Brandon raves about In-N-Out (they didn't have them in the "Show-Me State"). He also raves about Sarah.

"I'm her half-brother, technically. Same dad, different mom. I lived with my mom and hers died, so she lived with Dad. We were close, in a weird way, you know?"

Simon nods, though he doesn't know. He has no brothers or sisters.

"I hadn't kept in touch in a while, but I was planning on surprising her by visiting this weekend. I knew it was her birthday. Man." He shakes his head. "I dealt with the cremation and cleaning out her stuff. Man, she had a lot of pictures of you. She was a big fan, you know? I hope that doesn't freak you out."

"No more so, I guess, than her ghost visiting me at the studio lot."

"Her spirit. Not her ghost."

"Right, sure."

"No, there's a big difference. You see, a ghost doesn't know they're dead. A spirit is just visiting. By the way, I'm sure she didn't mean for you to jump in after her. She probably thought you knew."

"She probably thought I knew what?"

"I don't know, that I was throwing her ashes and that she was a spirit. She had to jump you know, join her ashes with her spirit, so she can be resurrected."

Simon, with three broken fingers, a chipped tooth, a sprained wrist, and a break in his ankle that will never, ever heal, nods and takes a huge bite of his burger. He speaks with his mouth full:

"Brandon, this is the most incredible thing that has ever happened to me. I can't even start to list how many ways my concept of reality has just gone whammo, ka-blooey, boom! It is just inconceivable!"

Simon looks into the heavens, which is presently the roof of his car, and marvels, "This is the biggest story of my life!... This... This... This *is* the story of my life!"

IT'S NOT ME

BY THE WAY, I'M NOT SARAH. Not anymore. Not at all. Maybe I never was. It's so strange to even think about that at all, now.

Who I was.

Who I am.

BRING IT

IF ONE IS A LITERALIST, "bring it" means one physically carries intended object to intended destination.

If one is at all hip to colloquialisms, one knows full well that to "bring it" means to bring one's entire being of mental, physical, spiritual and social abilities and graces to the task at hand.

Simon Would is all too hip.

He is going to take this tip, this piece of paper, and he is going to follow the given advice. He has three names, three leads. He is going to bring it: give him three leads, he'll find three stories.

He reads the note again:

Dear Mr. Would,

It would mean a great deal if you would please investigate the strange so-called 'suicide' of Sarah While. Talk to Adam Heath (lives in Hollywood); Frank Tudor

(Studio City) or Detective Walter Dervish (in Venice). They will have meaningful information for you. This is not 'a piece of cake'! It is a bloody mess!

    Love,

    An adoring fan

DERVISH

DETECTIVE DERVISH IS A SOFT-SPOKEN DARK BLACK MAN with a sweet-sized paunch that he carries in front of him like he's pregnant with his life-style, and perhaps he is. He wears it well. When Simon goes to his office, he moves them to a more private room.

"You know," Dervish says. "I have about twenty dead black girls in the past year that don't seem to merit a write-up in the *Times*, much less a book. Is suicide that much more literary than homicide?"

"I thought this was a homicide," Simon says.

Dervish shakes his head back and forth. "I don't know who's been doing your fact-checking."

Simon's mouth corners turn up. "I looked at your report, Dervish. I don't know who's been drawing your conclusions."

Dervish chuckles. He likes Simon. Most everyone likes Simon who isn't completely intimidated by him. "You're a handsome man,

Mr. Would. Most journalists are all...," he moves his hand across his face. "Pock-marked."

"You're an attractive man yourself. For a detective."

"Yes I am." Says Dervish, touching his belly. "My wife still thinks so, anyway. Should have seen me when I was your age. Could probably beat you one-on-one back then, too."

"Probably," says Simon.

Dervish sits down with a tired air. "So, what do you want from me? You have the report. You got the pictures?"

Simon nods, but Detective Dervish sails the dead-shot across the desk anyway. There she is in black and white — black where the blood still flowed out of the huge crosses on her wrists, floating. Shouldn't float. Two small bruises on her chest and one on her forehead, like she had been pressed down into the water and yet miraculously floated back up. Simon traces the outline of her face. It is so serene, she is almost smiling.

There is something so natural-looking about her face in death. There's something so alive.

"We consider this, you know, a case-closed suicide," Dervish says.

"With all the unusual circumstances?"

"Suicide is always rather unusual, isn't it? And as I stated before, we have twenty bona-fide homicides of young pretty ladies within the area who have definite killers which are solvable."

"You consider this unsolvable?"

"Well, if it's a suicide, it's already been solved."

"Homicide?"

"Then it's a magic trick, if you ask me. And I don't know a damn thing about magic, Mr. Would." Dervish stands up. "I'm gonna go outside and have a smoke."

"May I join you?"

"You smoke?"

"Why not? It won't kill me or anything."

Dervish laughs and gestures him outside.

It is bright and brilliant. A windstorm last night cleared all the smog. Dervish squints in the sun.

"Forgot my sunglasses," he says, lighting a Marlboro red. He offers one to Simon who takes it. "Seriously, son. They assign you this story cause it's freaky? Cause she's young white and pretty? What?"

Simon doesn't respond, too busy trying to find something to start his cigarette, and of course, he doesn't smoke and has nothing.

"Who sent you here?" Dervish asks, giving him a spark to start his small fire.

"I...," Simon inhales, thinking he can't tell Dervish the truth. "I can't reveal my sources," he says, finally.

"That's fine," says Dervish, dragging on his smoke and squinting in the sunlight. "You tell me this. You got a thing for the dead girl?"

Simon shakes his head violently, trying not to cough and get out "No, sir."

"Why are you lying?"

Simon takes a long drag on the cigarette, remembering the times in his life he has smoked, doing his best to look cool. "I just want to help, sir."

Dervish nods, thinking.

"You married, son?"

"Yes," Simon says.

"Kids?"

"A little girl. Six."

"That's nice. I got four of my own. Mostly grown, now." Dervish sends a long plume of smoke into the air, blinking at the sky's brightness. He is quiet for a few drags. Then:

"I understand where you're coming from. I do. I just want to make sure you know what you're getting into. I can't get into it, not now. Maybe when I was your age. But you've got a wife and a kid. You love them?"

"Of course."

"Not 'of course.' Plenty of boys don't know what they're doing, just get hitched and get involved in business they have no business being in. You a good daddy?"

"I'd like to think so."

"I'm sure you would, but that doesn't answer my question."

"Yes," says Simon. "I'm a good 'daddy.'"

Dervish puts out his cigarette. "Then you have no business getting into this shit. Stick with what you know. Gimme that." He takes the cigarette from Simon's hand, nearly burning him in the process and stamps it out. "Go home, son."

Simon stands there, looking at Dervish, feeling suddenly naked and shamed, like he's about to throw a temper tantrum, hitting and crying and thrashing around. He wishes that he were Dervish's 'son.' He wishes that he *could* just go home, that it were true that he had no business with this shit. Why was he not Dervish's son? Why could that not be?

Why instead, did he have a father who worked as a Man in Suit, a man who served in the telling of all types of secrets that he took to the grave. Why, his Father, who was so white he looked like he had no skin—like an invisible man upon first sight—why that? And why must his mother, his protection, leave him to that shark who would take him, silently, into a world that was his 'birthright'?

His Father was dead, and he thanked God when he died. He surely thanked God when that man was burned into ashes and scattered on the water and he was through and finished except for the money, the trail of money which his Father had left him—which provided him with his birthright, an education, an association of people. Did not his wife, his family, everything he now held dear, descend from that sulfur trail?

If he went 'home' as Dervish had said, would he not be forever falling back behind the Men in Suits, whose name and purpose he felt but could not name, who even still held him hostage? And Sarah—Sarah who floated with airless lungs, Sarah who bled when she had no blood, Sarah who wrote letters when she had no hands, who sang when she had no throat, who lived when she had no life—Sarah was the answer, he knew that more surely than he'd ever known anything.

Love, after all, can never die. And perhaps he was too late, or she was too late, to be able to see each other face to face, in life, in love. But it was not too late for him to love her. And it was not too late for him to save her, somehow, or for her to save him.

"You all right, son?" Simon is on the concrete, facing up into the sky. God, it was so bright. Had he fallen down? He doesn't remember falling. Had he hit his head? He had. A spot of red blood on the concrete.

"You fainted," says Dervish. "I didn't catch you. Sorry, son. I'm real sorry." He is sorry, too. Simon can tell. Maybe Dervish wishes the same thing, that he had been Simon's father, that he could have made it so he could go to a home that was a home, not some elaborately carved white lie with teeth.

"I have to help her," Simon says, choking on his own breath. "Please. You have to help me help her." Dervish nods at him with concern, love — a type of fatherly love that makes Simon start crying.

"All right, son," Dervish says, holding him, rocking him, like a child. "All right."

Simon sits in Dervish's office, a paper towel from the men's room, dripping wet, at the back of his head. The water keeps running down the back of his shirt and making him shiver, but is not altogether unpleasant. It keeps him focused.

Dervish writes on a dry-erase board using red, purple and blue markers. *Red,* apparently, indicates approximate time for events. *Purple* indicates facts. *Blue* means speculation. *Red*: 6:00 p.m., Tuesday, March 13th. *Purple*: Sarah leaves Brighton Research Center.

Red: 6:33 p.m. *Purple*: Sarah purchases sunglasses and a pack of cigarettes from the corner convenience store. Corroborated by employee, Ahmed Zrikaski, and the receipt from Sarah's bankcard, which she used and left at the site, with her wallet, which contained forty dollars cash. (Underlined by Dervish with a meaningful glance at Simon, like this proved something. Simon felt like he was failing some cognitive test — what was that supposed to signify?).

Red: 6:45-7:15 p.m. *Blue:* Sarah arrives home.

Red: 9:00 p.m. *Blue:* Neighbors in Apartment across alley hear Sarah start singing, very loud.

Red: 9:00 p.m. *Blue:* Downstairs neighbor, Ethel (does not hear singing) hears water running in Sarah's apartment.

Red: 9:00 p.m. *Purple*: The electricity goes out in Sarah's apartment building.

Red: 9:30 p.m. *Purple:* Building Manager comes to turn electricity back on in building. *Blue:* Sarah singing continues, according to neighbors across alley. Water still running according to Ethel.

Red: 9:45 p.m. *Purple:* Ethel's apartment roof and walls start leaking.

Red: 9:48 p.m. *Purple:* Ethel knocks on Sarah's door. No answer.

Red: 9:55 p.m. *Purple:* Building Manager opens Sarah's door.

Red: 9:56 p.m. *Purple:* Building Manager and Ethel find Sarah's body in tub.

Red: 2:00 a.m. *Blue:* According to neighbors, singing stops.

"Now," says Dervish. "What do you make of it?"

"This is pretty much what the report said, though it left out the singing bit."

"Right," says Dervish. "It makes no sense."

"Maybe it was somebody else singing," suggests Simon.

"Maybe they had their nights wrong," Dervish agrees.

"Either way, their story doesn't match up to anything. They could have heard a radio."

"Not from Sarah's building," corrects Dervish.

"Why?"

"No electricity."

"Right," says Simon.

"Maybe it was battery operated," says Dervish with a wink.

"So why isn't it in the report?"

Dervish gives him a wide sardonic grin. "Facts don't fit, leave it out of the report."

"That's pretty shoddy detective work," Simon says.

Dervish tosses his hand at him. "I'm a pretty shoddy detective. If you want those facts, you can use them. Say her ghost started singing and didn't stop tell after the bars closed, for all I care. Also, she sang and smoked at the same time. An entire pack of Reds. For a girl who supposedly didn't smoke."

"Interesting."

"Right. I've been smoking for twenty-five years. I couldn't down a pack in two hours unless I wanted to die right after."

"Maybe someone helped her smoke them," Simon suggests.

"And again, no signs of any break in, no sign of forced entry, no one saw anyone come or leave the building."

"But then again, the electricity was off."

Dervish gives him a meaningful pause and puts a finger on his nose.

"Why the underline treatment?" Simon says, pointing back at the underlined cash amount.

"Well, why does a lady pay for something with a bank card when she has cash?"

"Maybe she needed the cash for something else?"

"And why does she leave the wallet, after she pays?"

"She forgot it?"

"Maybe."

"Well, what are you suggesting?"

Dervish sits and gives a small shrug. "I think maybe she wanted to leave a little trail. Pay with a bankcard to prove she was there. Leave her wallet so they will try and find her."

"She knew she was going to be killed?"

"Or kill herself, more likely. It's the suicides that want the attention. Most people aren't privy to their own homicide."

Simon stares up at the ceiling, his head swimming. "This is a goddamn mess."

"You're telling me. Sure you don't want to call it quits? No hard feelings?"

Simon is so far past that consideration he barely even hears Dervish. "Did they say what she was singing?"

"Come again, son?"

"The neighbors across the alley. Did they say what they heard her singing?"

Dervish chuckles. "You are talking about six hours of singing, son. I think they listed a few in their witness accounts. They did say she sang *'Misty'* for them more than once."

Simon shivers. The dripping of the paper towel has become too much. He throws it into the trashcan, a huge brown red-headed spitball.

"How's the head?" Dervish asks. "Maybe you should get it looked at."

"It's fine."

Dervish slides a large manila envelope across his desk. "Here's your police report, the picture of the dead girl, and four witness accounts." He erases the board and turns his back to Simon.

"This is mine?" Simon asks, getting up, touching the envelope.

"Yep," says Dervish. "Mind your manners."

"You have another copy?"

"Shit," says Dervish. "Of course I do. I knew you were coming, boy."

"How'd you know something like that?" asks Simon.

Dervish touches the center of his forehead. "I got the touch, you know?"

Simon smiles. He doesn't believe in the touch, still, might as well give it a whirl.

"Then, there really isn't any mystery, sir. Just tell me how she died."

Dervish shakes his head. "No, son. That ain't none of my business to ask, and less of my business to tell."

Simon holds the manila envelope to his chest. "I thought that was precisely your business, sir. You are, in fact, a detective."

Dervish motions to him, curling his index finger. "I'm gonna whisper something to you, Simon Would. Come close, now."

Simon leans across the desk one direction, as Dervish leans the other. They meet in the middle, close enough to kiss. Dervish lightly turns his cheek and whispers in his ear: "Ask the typewriter."

"I'm sorry?" says Simon.

Dervish pats his cheek, and pulls back to behind his desk. "Go on now, son. Get out of here."

"I don't understand," says Simon. "

"You will," says Dervish, his face stern. "Get out."

MY OLD FRIEND, ADAM

"ADAM HEATH IN HOLLYWOOD," Simon says to the recorded AT&T voice. He is immediately given a number, but waits to talk to the operator to get an address.

Simon drives down near the blue Gotham Scientology center to where Adam Heath lives in a crumbling adobe duplex. He knocks on the door at twelve in the afternoon and receiving no answer he goes in for a closer look. He peers through a curtain-less window to spot a large bong and plenty of beer bottles.

He walks to the nearby Jack in the Box to wait and orders a Sourdough Jack and a Dr. Pepper. He reads his horoscope. When was Sarah's birthday? These were the sort of facts he had on his legal pad, which for some reason he left at home keeping his Dictaphone company. He shakes his head at his own shoddy reporting. Let's see, she died on her birthday which was Ides of March fare, making her a Pisces.

Her horoscope reads: "A new friend makes a meaningful commitment in the next two days. Be patient."

His horoscope, Sagitarius, reads "Do not disregard the significance of anything. In matters of love, keep it quiet."

Now that's a cryptic reading. "Keep it quiet"? Who's the quack who writes this drivel? Ah, Edna Hobokoppin. He's met her. He remembers how her wide eyes rolled around in her head like a dolls', closing like a shark about to bite. Wonder what she would say about his beyond-the-grave romance?

After an hour and a half he walks back down Adam's street, noting the infestations of cats, the children playing in the street. In his sweet suit and sure gait, he would have drawn attention if attention was to be paid, but it is not, in this day and age; not in this neighborhood, anyway.

There is a bike in front of the apartment now, and music emanating from the inside. He knocks and the door opens. The smell of freshly smoked grass comes out in waves. Adam, apparently, a boy with brown dreads and blue, bloodshot eyes and a shayna punim, regards him with a head-nod.

"Adam Heath?" Simon asks.

"What can I do ya for, man?" he asks in deep voice with a kind smile.

"I was wondering if I might speak to you for a moment about Sarah While?"

His face drops, but he steps back and gestures inside to the smoky cave. "Oh, yeah. Please. I mean, are you the cops or something?"

"A reporter."

"Oh, yeah then. Definitely." He screws up his face in thought and looks at Simon closely, his face breaking into a shit-eating grin. "Wait a second... you're... you're... that guy..."

"Simon Would."

"Simon Would! Oh, man! You can definitely come in, man!"

He claps Simon on the arm and follows him inside, continuing to nod his head saying, "Whoa. Wow. Simon Would."

Simon sits down on the torn, stained couch. Adam offers him the bong; Simon politely shakes his head.

"I just got off work, so you don't mind if I do, right?" Adam asks, already sparking the chamber.

"Not at all."

"Cool," says Adam, sucking in a great hit of smoke.

Simon looks around the apartment, once again amazed that he'd brought nothing to write on—what was his horoscope? "Disregard no detail"? Ah, if only he had a photographic memory.

Adam smokes Blue American Spirits, and eats—according to the accumulated fast food wrappers, mostly Taco Bell. Strange with the Jack-In-The-Box right around the corner. Probably a vegetarian.

His cheap plastic bookshelves are nearly collapsing with Hunter S. Thompson, Charles Bukowski, Fydor Dostovesky, and Anne Tyler.

"Simon Would. Man...," Says Adam again, releasing a dragon's wealth of smoke.

"You were a friend of Sarah's?" Simon asks

Sad face again. "For sure, man. You writing about her?"

"Yes."

"That would make her really, really happy, man. She was way into your writing. Seriously, man. She had everything you'd ever written ever, and she cut it out of the newspapers and like, make us all read it. That article you wrote about the legalization of drugs... that was dope."

Now that makes Simon laugh. Adam laughs too, like he made

the wordplay on purpose, and who knows, maybe he did. Simon already has pegged him as that smart, weird kid in school who took the "loser" track rather than the "sucker" track.

Simon, self-aware enough to know he is often on the fence between "winner" and "sucker", has a deep respect for those who let the baby have its bottle and take their own road. Not that he wants to sit around and smoke bong loads with the dude, but Sarah liked him, and he seems of a strange intelligence, like the pot smoke was a curtain behind which he hid some quiet brilliance.

"How do you think Sarah died?"

Adam nearly drops the bong and something completely shocking falls from his mouth. "She was murdered," he says.

"By whom?" Simon asks.

Adam shakes his head. "You won't believe me, man."

"Try me."

Adam tries him. "The Men in Suits."

"The Men in Suits?"

"Yeah. These guys—they travel in threes—Sarah called them the 'Men in Suits.' I don't know their actual names."

"Who are they? Or who do they work for—or wait a second. Wait a goddamn second."

Suddenly, Simon has a splitting headache. He hasn't had a migraine since he was a kid. He holds the bridge of his nose and tries to breathe. Like fingers on a chalkboard, like chewing a piece of aluminum in a filling, this piercing unbearable—"Are you okay, man?" Adam is saying.

"Migraine," Simon blurts, trying to inhale, exhale, inhale, exhale.

"Smoke this," Adam wraps Simon's fingers around the bong. "Seriously, smoke this. It will help. They prescribe it for migraines.

I used to get these wicked ones..."

And Simon finds himself actually inhaling the smoke, exhaling the smoke, and the pain dissipates in a breeze of Mary Jane. It is better.

He sits back on the couch. "The—uh—'Men in Suits,'" Simon says, coughing. And he is afraid. He is afraid of the Men in Suits.

He has always been afraid of them. He feels like he has a picture of them in his head that he does not want to see, but there they are, paper white men in dark black suits, always with sunglasses covering their eyes. Do they really have eyes? They are not really men, after all. They're spooks, demons, ghosts, wraiths. They cut into his thoughts like glass. They are cold and dead. They can't be real. Jesus.

He puts his head back on the couch and Adam touches his arm. "Do you want a drink, man? Some water? A beer? A shot of whiskey?"

Simon has forgotten why he came here in the first place. Has he always been here? Where is here? Who is clapping him on the arm? He thinks, "Oh, it is my old friend Adam. I love Adam." But he does not know Adam, he reminds himself, he just came here for... for Sarah.

Simon says, "I came here for Sarah." He opens his eyes and looks at Adam.

"I know, man. And I know that she is so glad you did. She really loved you, man. You were her hero."

"I find that strange," Simon says. "I've never done anything heroic."

"That's not true," Adam says. "Right now, man. What you are doing right now." Simon looks into Adam's face. It is a beautiful face. He feels all right, now. Good. He is good. Yes. Simon feels loved, safe, Sarah. He feels Sarah.

"I love Sarah," Simon says.

"Yes," Adam says. "I know."

Adam gets him a mug of water with two ice cubes melting at the top. Simon drinks it, feels like weeping but he is not sad. He feels like something inside of him is healing. Happy.

"What do you do, Adam?" he asks.

"Oh, this, mostly," says Adam. "I also ride my bike. Do bike messages. That's how I make some cash, stay in shape. You?"

"I'm a journalist."

"Right. Yeah. How do you stay in shape?"

"Oh I lift weights at the gym. Play some basketball."

"You any good?"

"Oh, yeah. Real good."

"Yeah," says Adam, like that's what he was expecting.

Simon drinks some more water and looks around the apartment. It was dark when he came in, but now light streams through the window, and he can see the dissipating smoke carrying colors and particles of dust. He is part of this—the smoke, the light, the dancing particles.

"The Men in Suits." Simon says.

"The Men in Suits. Yeah," says Adam. "They travel in threes. They aren't really men. Spooks, really."

Simon knows. "White skin, black suits."

"Sunglasses. Who knows if they really have eyes."

"Demons."

"Maybe."

"Who do they work for?"

Adam shrugs.

"Why did they want Sarah?"

Adam looks at him, sustaining a puzzled look. "Why do they want *you*?"

SIMON STARTS TO LOSE IT

SIMON'S ONCE UPON A TIME HOME is an immaculate manifestation of taste, grace and success. He owes this all to his lovely wife, Lucy. Lucy is half-asian, half-caucusian, with perfect almond eyes with flecks of green. She has small delicate bones and silken skin. She was born and raised in San Diego, went to Vassar and then was awarded her Master's in Art History from Princeton.

She knows art.

Thus, his home, in the lovely Beverlywood area, has some of the most original and beautiful found art as well as tasteful but little-known prints from Picasso, Manet, Van Gogh, Rembrant. Guests don't know they're Picasso, Manet, Van Gogh and Rembrant, so that she can tell them, while they are sipping Chateau Neuf de Pap and eating brie on rice wafers, "Oh yes, obscure, but one of my favorites."

His walls are of delicate hues, his hard wood floors polished and gleaming, his carpets lush and clean. She works at a gallery on Melrose and can discuss his work with him in an informed, educated and always enlightening manner. She is the ultimate and perfect match for his life choice. She is warm, caring, a wild-cat in bed, and they have a daughter about to enter kindergarten who is the light of his life and probably the most gorgeous being ever conceived, if he does say so himself.

He has, on occasion, dabbled in the cheating arts, gotten cozy with a starlet, cozened with a model, petted an up and coming ingenue. These dalliances he does not report back to the lovely Lucy, though he is sure she would forgive him, for she is very forgiving. Telling her would be in poor taste. He has seen enough turtle-necked, designer-spectacled artists with their hands on her just-so in a public, platonic show of gratitude to know that he is probably not alone in needing to ask forgiveness for being 'human' (as the song goes).

They both know that their affairs are altogether meaningless in a marriage of mutual respect, admiration and suitability. Ariella is the main focus of both of their lives and they discuss endlessly which school is most appropriate for her, which activities most beneficial, which friends most winsome. It is a lovely life Simon Would is living, far more lovely than he ever would have imagined for himself, and he is, after all, grateful.

He thanks the heavens (why not?) when he enters his home and goes immediately to the shower to wash off the smell of smoke and the smell of Sarah. (The smell of Sarah? Yes, he can smell her lilac perfume, something animal and sweet, like he would imagine hay would smell, on his fingertips, in his hair. Strange, yes strange).

Lucy comes in as he is soaking beneath the massage head, asking if he would like to go out for to a nice dinner and get Julie to come sit for Ariella.

"Smashing," he says in his British accent, which he busts out for Lucy who loves the Brits. It is another perfect evening for Simon Would.

Later he is lying in his bed as Lucy reads *The Economist* next to him. He tries to clear his mind of everything but his own perfect life—the blessings that have been given to him.

He finds himself tracing back to his childhood—not much of a childhood, but it's over—his mother's death—the appearance of his father like a ghost in the church.

"That's daddy," Grandma says, pointing to the only white man. "He's going to take care of you, now." Yes, the first time he saw his father was at his mother's funeral. He was The Man in the Suit—but you could see his eyes, and there was only one of him.

"What are you working on now?" Lucy asks, turning the page in the periodical.

"HMO's. Cover story," he lies, turning over in the bed to face the wall. Beige.

"Good. I don't like it when they assign you those fluff pieces. You've worked too long and too hard for that."

"Hmm?" he says.

"I don't mean 'fluff.' What's the word you always use?"

"Spook?"

"Right. It's just not your area of expertise. Tragedies and crime stories I mean. If you want to move into that field I suppose it's all right, but I think you're better at the political, legal action stories. You know?"

"Yes, indeed. Who wants to spend their time talking to cops and criminals and the bereaved?"

"Exactly. Did you finish the article already?"

"Which, now?"

"About the dead girl. In Venice."

"Sarah."

"We're on a first name basis, now?" she says, hitting him with The Economist and a smile.

He says nothing.

"Have you finished it?" she asks, again.

"No."

"Is someone else finishing it?"

Simon makes a "no idea" face.

Lucy is quiet for a moment, staring at his back and taking in the silence.

"Anyway, why don't you write another book? You liked that, last time."

"Yes, I did."

"It's about time, again. Don't you think?"

"I do."

"Maybe this HMO piece—is it a cover story?"

"Should be."

"Maybe that will springboard you. We need a good book on health care. It can be like that—oh what was that book written about the mental institutions that caused all that social reform...?"

"I'm going to go check on Ariella," Simon says.

He gets out of bed, feeling the whisper of his purple silk boxers against his thighs. He walks down the hallway, the polished wood floor gleaming up at him as his bare feet pad softly. *Once in a Lifetime* lyrics appear uninvited in his head. "This is not my beautiful house. This is not my beautiful wife."

Ariella's door is slightly ajar, the way she likes it to be to fall asleep. He nudges the door open. The white noise machine (also to help her sleep; the child has never been an easy sleeper) greets him with its soft "Earth Sound" setting: the sound of water and birds. Ariella sleeps in her small bed. Her comforter is thick and decorated with the sun, the moon and the stars. A friendly faced-giraffe, chimpanzee, and flamingo twirl lightly on a mobile string above her bed and cast fairy-tale shadows on the wall.

Simon marvels at this room. They have created this for her, this perfect cocoon of childhood. He listens to Ariella breathe, soft, even breaths and make this place real. He touches her head. He feels so lucky, he cannot believe it.

"Thank you, gentle spirit," he says to the sleeping girl, incredulous that he has said such a thing as soon as it has left his mouth. This is not him.

He hasn't been stoned in a while. Perhaps getting high has released this onslaught of new-agey gratitude and lingo.

A week ago, he'd been bitter he wasn't going overseas.

Ariella moves her lips in her sleep.

Simon crouches next to her to hear. Will she talk in her sleep?

He has never known her to talk in her sleep, but then again, he has never really paid attention.

Her lips move and she says, distinctly, "Sarah."

He waits for her to say something else, but she says nothing, continuing to breathe evenly in harmony with the "Earth Sound" around her.

"You're up early," Lucy shoots at Simon. Ariella is eating breakfast and crying because Lucy won't let her take her doll to school. It is an expensive doll, not really for playing with, Lucy explains. Certainly not for taking to school and besides Mrs. Matthieson has told them not to bring toys except on show and tell.

Simon hangs in the doorway, in his silk robe, a strange look on his face.

"You want coffee?" asks Lucy. Their housekeeper and nanny, Juanita, pours him a mug before he can answer.

"Eggs? Toast?" Juanita asks him.

Lucy walks out of the room; she has not yet "put on her face." She touches his arm on her way out. "Busy day ahead?" she says without waiting for any answer.

Simon walks, holding his cup of coffee out ahead of him, careful not to spill, his eyes on his child. He sits down next to her as she rips her toast apart into little pieces.

"Good morning, Daddy," she says.

"Good morning, Sunshine," he says. Does he usually call her Sunshine? It feels funny in his mouth.

"May I please take Susie to school?" Ariella asks him.

"Who's Susie?" he asks.

"That doll," says Juanita, pointing to a perfect China Doll sitting in the chair opposite Ariella.

Simon is washed over with relief. She must have said "Susie" in her sleep. Not "Sarah." He heard "Sarah" because he had that name on the brain.

"Did you dream about Susie last night?" he asks.

Ariella shakes her head, pinching her face at him. "I want to take her to school."

It's a five hundred dollar doll, but what are dolls for if not to play with—even such expensive ones? It was his bum idea to buy it for her in the first place.

"Well, I don't see what's wrong with that," Simon says, sipping his coffee.

"Uh-oh," says Juanita. "You best just go back to bed, Mister Would."

It is not a bad idea.

He puts the coffee mug on the table and says, "Well, do what your mother says."

Ariella lets out a wail.

"What? What? What?" Simon says, unused to the sound of Ariella screaming at him. He usually gets nothing but the sweet Ariella. He always plays Good Cop, after all.

"I need her! I need her!" she screams.

"Why? She'll be here when you get home!"

"She keeps away the Bad Men!"

"What Bad Men?"

"The Bad Men who follow me!"

"You're being followed? Have you told your teacher?"

Lucy walks back into the room, brushing her hair and Simon grabs her roughly by the arm. "She says she's being followed! Jesus Christ! Have you talked to the teacher or the cops or—"

Lucy pulls her arm back and hits him on the hand with her brush.

"What is wrong with you?" she whispers. "You're scaring her!"

Ariella watches them both with wide-eyes. Juanita is frying eggs like nothing is happening at all.

"She says she's being followed by 'Bad Men'. That doesn't alarm you?"

"She had a nightmare last night. Don't you dare encourage her to think her nightmares are real, asshole."

"Where did you see the Bad Men?" Simon demands of his child.

Ariella starts nodding. "Asleep. I was dreaming. I didn't see them outside. I just want Susie!" She starts crying.

"See? See?" Lucy says, rushing over to Ariella.

"She can take the goddamn doll to school, goddammit!" Simon

says, hitting the doorframe with his fist. The kitchen is silent except for the sound of grease popping in the frying pan. "You understand, Lucy?" He turns around to face her. His teeth are slightly bared and his whole body is tense, and pulled back, like he might pounce. "She can take the doll to school!"

"Fine," Lucy manages to say, though her face is expressionless with shock.

Simon hits the doorframe again and walks out of the room.

Lucy looks at Ariella, expecting her to burst into tears, tears she herself are barely holding back.

But Ariella is eating her toast, as if Simon lost his temper every day; as if she had seen that man who shouted and pounded his fists in the doorway before.

Lucy never had.

FUNNY GUY

SIMON HAS BROUGHT IT, ALL RIGHT. He looks again at the letter left by 'an adoring fan'. He has his suspicions (or his hopes) as to who left this letter. "Ask the typewriter," Dervish had said. His fingers play across the slightly-raised type-written characters. He reads it again and again like a poem. He's contacted Dervish and Adam. There's just one name left: Frank Tudor.

Frank Tudor's address is not listed, or rather, it's listed as "Unlisted." Unsure of what to do next, Simon finds himself at his agent's office, proposing a book about the death of Sarah While. His agent is all gaga in his typical modus operandi.

"Simon!" he says in that *I'm not leaving until I sell you something!* voice. "Simon, I can't tell you how excited and thrilled, yes, thrilled about this new venture! I mean, I think it's great! People are going to eat it up! Local girl, weird freaky cult death. Who knows? Maybe she killed herself! Drugs, dancing, she's hot—we can put pictures in the book, right? Pictures of her home, the apartment. Can we get a picture of her dead?"

Simon nods. The picture of her floating when she shouldn't float is floating in his brain, where it also shouldn't float. He's thinking she is Snow White, and if he had got to her in time and kissed her she would have awakened. It's wrong. It's disgusting. He is still nodding and the phone is ringing.

"Hold on a second, Simon." His agent has to take a call. Simon picks up his agent's squishy stress ball and leafs through a stack on his desk.

Sitcom pilots. And a head-shot, of all things, of Frank Tudor. The guy has a real Fozzie Bear look. Goofy Glasses. Goofy Hair line. Goofy expression. Wakka-wakka.

The agent gets off the phone and says, "So, where are you, now, with the story?"

"Who's this guy?" Simon asks, waving the head-shot.

"Frank Tudor. My partner's really pushing this guy into the literary game. He's written a couple of television pilots. He's a stand-up comic, does commercials. You know, if you're interested, you might get in on it. It's not really your bag, but..."

"I'd like to meet him. ASAP."

"Sure, well, I'll see what I can do."

"I need to see him now. Today."

Frank meets Simon at a swanky 24 hour breakfast nook. He looks, as is typical, completely different than his head-shot. Fozzie Bear is replaced by a beaten and desperate looking character with a cynicism around the eyes that is only funny when they are narrowed and impersonating. He orders a bottled water and then excuses himself to the bathroom. When he comes back, he rubs his eyes and blows his nose.

"Excuse me," he says. "I've just lost my second wife."

"I'm terribly sorry," Simon says, thinking this is a lot of death to be thrown upon some guy in a month.

"Yeah. To a fucking bricklayer, if you can imagine. A fucking blue collar working class hero. Of course, she'll try and get half. She won't get half. I have a damn good lawyer. Oh, well. Third time's the charm, huh? Know any nice girls? And I mean—" he makes a curvy body pantomime with both hands "—Nice?"

He laughs at his own joke.

Simon's face is still.

Frank takes in his tough audience. "Right, well. So, Larry says you might be interested in helping me with this pilot. You're some writer of some sort. Some established, money-making, well-respected writer sort, yes?"

"I suppose so."

Frank shifts in his seat like he's about to sell some great pyramid scheme. "Now, my name has a lot of pull. My face has a lot of pull. I would be starring in the pilot, of course."

"Actually, I'm not here about the pilot. I just asked to meet you."

Frank makes a 'to-charm' face and crosses his legs. "A fan? Like the way I sell a McDonald's cheeseburger? Have your own little project you can't wait to get my hands on?"

Come to think of it, now that he's staring right at him, Simon does recognize him. "Actually, it's about Sarah."

Frank's face immediately drops, but he says, "Sarah? Sarah who?"

"Sarah While."

Frank nods. He doesn't say anything for a minute, just stares at the bottled water, then picks it up in his hand, watches it for a moment as it moves.

"You knew her?" Simon asks.

"Knew her? In what sense, knew her?" Frank says, in a bitter tone under his breath. "Clinically? Casually? Biblically? Yes. All three. I knew her." He still stares at the water. Then he looks at Simon, accusing. "How did you know?"

"I'm an investigative reporter. I don't reveal my sources."

"Like a private dick, huh?"

"Maybe."

Frank practically spits at him as he says, "Private dick, right. You fucked her?"

"I didn't know her," Simon says, his face and tone calm.

"Your loss, buddy." Frank drains the water, impressively, like it were twelve shots of whiskey and he the jonesiest alcoholic in the world. Then he points a well—manicured finger at Simon. "She knew you," he says.

"How do you mean?" Simon asks.

"It's just like her," Frank says. "Maybe she staged this whole Polanski death scene just to get you. You ever think of that?"

"It hadn't occurred to me."

"Well, there's another thing for you to investigate." Frank's face pulls in like a shrew's, his tone as bitter as black burnt coffee three days old. "You see her room?"

Has he seen her room? He feels as if he has, but of course... "No."

"I'm sure they cleaned it out. She had framed photos of you." Frank voice takes on a quick and dirty conspiratorial tone. "Kissed them at night," he says, his eyes gleaming.

"Do you mind if I record our conversation?" Simon pats the Dictaphone in his pocket, not yet unsheathed.

"I guess I do mind," Frank says. "As I said before, under a previous guise of this meeting, my name, you see, I don't want my name associated with..." He makes a strange gesture: touching his wrists then nose and then pushing out his hands.

Simon goes cold. The gesture is...

As Frank calls over the waitress, flirting with her while ordering an egg white omelette, wheat toast, no butter, Simon tries to put it together. Wrists cut. Nose, suffocated? Pushing out hands—no thank you? The waitress turns to him and Simon orders the number 9, unsure exactly what it is but not ready to consult the menu. And coffee, cream, no sugar.

When the waitress walks away, Frank gives Simon an aside. "You must think I'm a terrible person, right?"

"I don't judge people," Simon says. "I try to be objective. Just get the story."

"Well, that will serve you, buddy. That will serve you just fine. Fact is, you want someone to put their name down, she's got a thousand freaky friends with nothing better to do than speculate on the nature of Sarah While's death. What the fuck do you need me for?"

Simon throws his hands up.

"You picking up this tab?" Frank asks.

"Of course," says Simon,

"Well then, let's just have a good breakfast. Your disappointment that you get no info can equal my disappointment that my pilot isn't in major development. You dig?"

"I dig," Simon is digging, knowing in knowing the way he knows these sorts of things, that this fish is hooked and will be spilling whatever guts he's got soon enough.

"Right. Where's that bitch with my coffee?"

Simon speculates that Frank is rarely at any sort of loss for words or conversational topics, and yet he is silent as he lays into the omelette. Then, after two cups of coffee Frank finally offers:

"Do you know about the therapist?"

Simon shakes his head.

"I referred her to my therapist, you know. We met at a party—she was really... odd. Strange girl. Wanted to be a singer. I told her, considering our... intimate time together, I felt... I'm a responsible guy, really, Mr..."

"Would."

"Right. Sorry, I know it's Simon Would. My mind keeps blanking. Don't be offended I didn't know you right away, either. Your name was familiar. Because of Sarah, mostly. She was a big fan. I just—there's a lot of names I have to remember."

"I'm not offended."

"Great. I hate it when people take offense. It makes me twitchy.."

"You're a responsible guy," Simon says, trying to bring him back.

"Sure am. I mean, I married two girls—not at the same time, mind you. Both because they were knocked up—both of whom lost the babies or lied to me, I don't know which and I don't really care. I provided for them. I try and do the right thing, I really do. So I wanted to help Sarah. She wanted to be a singer, you know."

"Yeah."

"Helping her was like pulling teeth. Always with the—" (and here, Frank pulls a squeaky girl voice from thin air that sounds vaguely insulting to whomever he was supposed to be impersonating, in this case, Sarah, and Simon is offended) "'I wouldn't feel right about that,' and 'I don't need to impress anyone.' Well, she did. You do. That's the nature of the business. Not all people are created equal, despite what your civil history course might say.

"You know, I get this big-time manager to some dive open mike night—an open mike night, mind you—and she sings, can you believe it—'*Misty.*' Like he's supposed to be able to market that. And she's a sexy girl, whoa, very sexy, and what's she wearing? A fucking like Holly Hobby dress, singing '*Misty*' like she's in church or something. Jesus. I mean, I had some explaining to do to that guy just to keep my creds with him, let me tell you."

Frank lays into whatever is left on his plate like he's trying to keep his creds with *It.*

"So what about the therapist," Simon asks.

"Right, the therapist. So she starts telling me shit about her childhood, like it's pillow talk or something—like it's fucking pillow talk for Jesus' sake—that would turn your hair white. I mean, Jesus. We all have fucked up family lives, but this stuff is just... way out of my league. And I'm all—you need to see a shrink, sweetie. She doesn't want to see a shrink, she doesn't trust shrinks, she's got bad associations with shrinks, which, if the shit she's telling me is true, I understand. And finally I'm like—this is my shrink and you need help. I even paid for her first three sessions as a fucking birthday gift. I'm like that, I'm responsible, I try to take care of people."

"Do you have any interest in relaying any of the childhood information to me?"

Frank chokes a little on his food and recovers. "No way, buddy. No fucking way. I've probably blocked most of it out by this point, anyway."

"Do you think I could talk to the therapist?"

An evil look creeps up Frank's face from the chin up. "Maybe. If he weren't dead."

Simon isn't sure what to say next.

"Are you going to eat anything or just stare at your hash-browns, buddy?" Frank says.

"How did the therapist die?"

"Nothing spectacular. Heart failure. He was like, sixty. Nice man. White hair, so no danger of Sarah's childhood doing any lasting damage to his coiffure."

"When did he die?"

"About two months ago. Sarah was real broken up about it, too. She saw him for almost a year. I think he had a sliding scale. She couldn't really afford him. He was the best, you know. She probably worked that last job so she could have benefits to afford him. That is so Sarah. What a nut-case."

Frank finishes his omelette in three huge bites. He reminds Simon of some large dog, affable enough to the owners, but vicious.

"Sweetie, more coffee?" he says, holding up his cup.

When the waitress refills the coffee, Simon feels a sudden panic. Frank isn't going to order dessert. Frank is finished with his omelette and Simon is paying the bill. Frank is about to leave, and with him, vaults of information. Simon has the sudden desire to beat the living shit out of him and then make him talk.

Simon sits, quite literally on his hands. He has a temper these past days he never had.

"Frank," he says, calmly. "You are a responsible man, I can see that. But I think that perhaps you are shirking your responsibility here. Something terrible has happened to someone you cared about, and I am trying to help her."

Frank lets out a guffaw. "That's funny. That really is."

Frank looks back into Simon's eyes, his own as intense and direct. His voice drops to a whisper, but moves with his eye-line. "She's dead, buddy. You can't help her anymore."

Frank stands up, not finishing his coffee.

"Would you like to take my card, in case you change your mind?" Simon asks, using his most winning smile.

"Hey, your agent knows my agent. I can find you, just like you found me." Frank throws down his napkin and actually says, "Happy Hunting. Wakka, wakka."

THE KEY IN HIS POCKET, WRITTEN ON THE INSIDES

SIMON SITS IN HIS CAR outside his home, the engine still running. Whatever he has, it is nothing he can fit into the boxes he knows how to shape into stories. Then again, he could make it work, could force-fold it into sense. If Sarah were mentally ill, then the Men in Suits are just part of her (and maybe his) sickness.

He thinks of what Dervish whispered to him, he thinks of the letter, the singing, the floating, these things that are outside the realm of natural and are dismissed. But what does it really matter?

How can he help her, now that she is dead?

He turns off the engine and pulls out the keys. He puts them in his pocket and his fingers absently touch a small rectangle.

Out of his pocket he pulls a nametag.

It has been used and folded.

It is like a love-note from a dream, that somehow made it across the sub to waking consciousness. Where did it come from? How did it get here? What does it mean?

It is a nametag with *her* name.

A piece of cake, he thinks, though he can't fathom why. A cake-walk.

What is it to love a ghost?

What is it to be loved back?

As he sits in his car, plummeting to the bottom of this thought *(there is no bottom)* Lucy pulls in behind him. But this bit of normalcy (his wife's car, he's home, she's home, everyone's *home* now for God's sake) does nothing to slow his descent. Lucy does not acknowledge him, perhaps she does not see him, sitting there in his car. But he watches her from the corner of his eye, her movement as she goes to the passenger back door to unbuckle Ariella, who is holding to her controversial doll, Susie. They go inside.

He should follow now; he should get out of his car and follow. Come on, now, this is his life.

What is it to be loved back?

Surface for air, Simon, or suffocate in that thought—it is madness.

He wills himself, forces himself, to open his car door and follow.

Lucy screams.

Simon runs inside to see.

The back window has been completely shattered... with a typewriter. Yes, it appears a typewriter is the culprit.

"What the fuck?" screams Lucy, clutching Ariella, who is clutching Susie.

"Simon, what the fuck? Call the cops!"

But Simon wants to laugh. He doesn't. He moves toward the

typewriter, which sits upright in the center of the floor like it is waiting to be questioned.

"Don't touch it!" screams Lucy, but Simon cannot help it. His fingers move over its broken metal body to the ribbon, which has been pulled out of its cartridge and spools on to the keys like a deflated backwards thought bubble. He cannot help holding it up to the light.

Backwards, the letters show through clear against the black powder.

It is all here, in fact, clear, intact, visible through the light, backwards.

.dnuora emit siht em

PART THREE-
TAKE IT

Wherein...

You take the couch.

Sarah comes down.

Sarah rolls.

And many things get broken.

THINGS GET BROKEN

THIS HAPPENS AFTER ALL THE MESSINESS that is about to ensue, ensues. This happens after Simon has decided to clean it all up, his mess and anyone else's mess that happened along the way.

A conservative estimate puts him at over a year of making a terrible mess of everything he touches. A liberal estimate gives him three.

He feels bad. He has hurt people he loves and people he barely knows. He has delighted in hurting them, because then they have something in common, he and they, because he has felt nothing but a terrible aching pain. What is it to search for answers so desperately and find none? (What is it to love a ghost?).

So he makes a decision. He has not found answers, so he will make them up. And make them up he does.

And then he cleans up. He takes a long bath, shaves for the first time in a week, and walks around his Loz Feliz condominium wearing a silk red kimono that was a gift from his ex-wife who he can barely remember at this point enough to miss. He is sober. He is like F. Scott Fitzgerald on the wagon, drinking nothing but Coca-Cola, but an impressive amount of that.

Now he is talking on his cell-phone to his agent about the book that is living in the trunk of his car. His agent says he will send a courier to pick it up later that morning, and Simon says no, he will hand-deliver it to his door, right now at one in the morning. Simon needs a good excuse to get out, to get dressed, to pretend he is a human being.

One in the morning is better than never.

He is holding a small blue glass filled with ice and Coca-Cola (from the can, his third can within the so far thirty minute conversation with his agent) and insisting "now, yes now," when everything drops from his hands.

The cell-phone flies from his grip across the floor and the small blue glass, filled with ice and Coca-Cola from the can, hits the counter and shatters in all directions.

"Fuck!" he cries out and goes for the phone, laughing at himself.

He tells his agent that he has to say good-bye now to clean up the goddamn mess. He will be over there shortly.

"I'm sorry," his agent says. After nearly a decade with Simon, he has learned to associate sorrow with Simon. "I know you wanted that Coke." (Simon had been rhapsodizing on its salubrious effects earlier in the conversation).

"It's fine," Simon says. "Things get broken."

It is important that Simon says this, a marker of the functionality of his healing process.

"Things get broken" has been a self-made mantra of sorts for Simon in understanding both the literal sense of how objects become pieces which are no longer of any utilitarian value, and the metaphorical sense in how relationships between people and within oneself can no longer work or exist.

Say, "Fuck it," clean up and move on, because things get broken in this world.

He puts down his cell phone and tries to step with his bare feet over the broken glass. This is impossible, for the small blue glass contains an infinite amount of clear blue shards. The Coke is like liquid brown glue. The ice is distinguishable from the glass only in shape, and in that it moves slightly across the floor.

He is pierced in the center of his left foot where he sometimes, sometimes not, limps. And then as he kneels down to pick up the largest piece of glass, the center of his right palm is sliced.

"What does it mean? What is the meaning? Why, now? What is it trying to say?" These thoughts white out all others, like a migraine begging for a purpose.

He tries to respond with his mantra, but "things get broken" doesn't cut it when he is bleeding so suddenly and violently from the hand and the foot.

Staring down at his blood running down his arm, the blue cut glass, the brown liquid, the red blood... "What does it mean? What does it mean? What does it mean?"

He didn't know. He doesn't know. He has to ask.

"Sarah," he says. "Sarah, please."

The lights go out.

He is shocked by the darkness—as black as when his eyes are closed at night—and he is shocked by her response.

He had never been afraid of her all this time, of her death, of her ghost, of how she had driven him toward madness.

But now, he *is* afraid. Now he is fear itself like the scream of a tree being sawed in two, fear because he isn't alone in here, fear because he knows she means for *him* to be broken.

He knows that whatever is left of her here means for him to bleed to death now, in the dark.

TAKE IT

IT'S THE SMALLEST THINGS that change everything... and nothing at all.

Somewhere you are on a beach. Somewhere you are in love. Somewhere you are being strangled by a pale man in sunglasses. What's the difference?

For you, it's just the choice of whether or not to take a free couch on the street. Remember?

"Take it."

You have the momentary sensation of a ticking in your brain and the uncomfortable freedom of being master of your fate. Do you risk being late for your corporate job for a free couch?

You decide, why not. Take it! It's free!

You place your keys and attaché case on the intended couch, pulling it from the end closest to your building. It is extraordinarily heavy and you can barely move it, never mind hoisting it up the stairs. You are about to give it up when a dread-locked dude rides by on his bike.

"Need some help?" he asks, slowing and putting out his foot as a kick-stand.

You shrug.

He offers you his hand. "I'm Adam."

"Richard," you say. (See! You've already made a friend!)

Despite the couch's weight, the two of you heave and haul it up your stairs, sweating and making grunting noises. It fits inside your front door through clever adjusting at various angles, nicking the paint on either side as you push it in.

"Where do you want it?" asks Adam.

"Uh..." (where *do* you want it?)

"How about against this window?" he says. "Good Feng Shui."

"Sure," you say, doubting the Feng Shui, but digging the location for viewing the television.

Congratulations. The couch almost makes your place look almost like somebody cool lives there. Almost.

"Well, I gotta get to work," you say since Adam seems in no hurry to leave.

"Sure thing," says Adam. "Take her easy."

You make your way to your Jeep. (Awesome wheels! Yeah, you're in effing Californ-I.A. now, man!).

You won't be that late for work. Turn that key, let's hear some tunes.

Your car won't start. You don't know a damn fool thing about cars, but it seems to you that if the engine is not turning over, the battery must be dead. Did you leave the lights on? No. Radio? No. It's just dead, that's all.

You look for biker dude with the nonsensical hope that he might have jumper cables (on a bike?), but he is long gone.

The neighbor from the first apartment in your building, a blue-collar, middle-aged black man walks out of his home, almost as if on cue.

"Car dead?" he asks.

"Yeah," you say.

"I got cables," he says. (Making friends right and left, you are. See how it works? You get a couch, you get friends to sit on the couch. I told you so).

The two of you get your car started soon enough and clap—shake hands on the deal. As your Jeep (still has "show me" state plates; gotta take care of that) rattles itself to life, your neighbor ("Bill" he said, while you were putting the plus to the + and the minus to the -) gives you a look and pats your shoulder.

"Rough couple of months?"

"I miss my mom and dad, I guess," you say. "My friends back home. But, you know. I'm adjusting."

"Any weird things happen?"

"Uh..." You are not quite sure what he means.

"Well," he says, as if he never asked, "I gotta go lay some concrete." He tips an invisible hat to you. You put the hood down, get in your Jeep, and drive up the block.

Pearl Jam is singing, "*Son, she said. Have I got a little story for you,*" and you turn it up. You are at a stop sign when the Jeep goes deader than dead.

You aren't a swearing man, by nature, but you emit some choice words. You have a AAA membership, but a mechanic's shop is right directly across the street. You push your Jeep over, steering the wheel through the rolled down window.

"Alternator," says the mechanic.

You could take a bus or a cab to work. The Blue Buses are supposed to be nice, clean but you are suddenly overwhelmed with an exhaustion nearing total break down.

You leave your Jeep and walk home and call in sick to work. Are you lying?

Didn't you just wake up and now you're tired again?

What's gotten into you, Rich? Do you have the flu?

Well, whatever you said vs. the truth, you are lying down right now on the couch, thinking you should have shampooed it, vacuumed it. Who knows how long it was outside and what crackhead made it his bed? But it smells nice — there is a smell like lilacs — reminds you of hide and seek as a child — you'd hide beneath the lilac bushes, laughing... your mommy's shoes walking right by asking, "Where's Richie? Where is he? Where did he go?"

And you are asleep, hands clasped to your chest, and boy, do you dream.

THE COUCH

THE THINGS HUMANS TYPICALLY CLASSIFY as "non-living" still absorb and emit a great deal of energy. You don't have to believe me, and if you do, I certainly wouldn't recommend obsessing over it (you can go soup to nuts over it pretty darn fast), but I do want to explain about the couch.

The couch was a favorite of mine. It was unbelievably heavy and extremely uncomfortable to sit and lie on. Although it was once-upon a time gorgeous, it was eventually run-down with its perpetual use as a two-cat scratching post. But gorgeous it remained in its essence. When I slept on it, it seemed like my dreams came from the couch itself—like it was a subconscious flying couch just as I was a subconscious flying person and we rode like Aladdin and his carpet to many "Whole New Worlds."

So, it is with the memory of this bulky weighty couch that I take you, in between story lines, on a funny "ha-ha" and funny "strange" tour of dreams. For whether I was on the couch, sleeping in my car, or lying in a right and proper bed, when that strange peace washed over me, I felt I could remember past lives, future feelings, meet and greet the cosmic elite both living and dead.

On that couch, with the wind blowing the curtains, the sun washing the carpet, blue smoke from the cigarette moving like a spirit, a contentment surrounded me like a light. Here I am. Here I will always be. This moment is eternal.

You are here, too. We blend, as we do in dreams, pronouns becoming confused as you are you and not you, me and not me, that person and still yourself. It is like this in dreams. You know that, don't you? How you can be someone else entirely and still it's you?

So it is, now. We are one.

DREAMS OF US

DREAMS OF US, me and you. You could remember them later. Maybe even in time to save you.

Your dream:

You are me, wearing my long black coat. The day is gray but you are wearing sunglasses. You are walking up the back-way to my apartment, and the parking lot attendant looks at you with his mouth agape.

He says my name and asks, "Is your soul at rest?"

"Yes," you say with my voice. "I'm just visiting." You realize you are impersonating a ghost.

"Come back," he says, and says my name. "Come back any time."

We both find it somewhat romantic that even dead, I am welcome.

You walk up the back staircase. The apartment door is missing the crucial pieces of what makes a door—hinges and a knob—and rests broken against the frame. The majority of the vertical blinds are missing except for one lonely blind that hangs, looking goofy, like a tooth in a toothless mouth.

Trash, clothes, shoes, two giant aquariums, ash-trays filled to the brim. A huge cage houses a green parrot, who remains inside even though the door to the cage, like the one to its apartment, is broken and open.

Windows are smashed.

Handfuls of tiny birds—finches, you think—cluster on the coffee table with the ashtrays and bedding that has been piled up there.

Someone broke in to feed my cats and set free the birds, but the birds came back.

You must take care of all the animals. You put my hand around a tiny red bird and feel its flutter on my palm. Your breath catches—my breath—and you open your eyes.

You wonder what happened to the animals.

"Who is taking care of my birds?" you ask.

It is a question the ghost would ask, but you are genuinely curious.

Wake up!

My dream:

I dream of a small boat, rolling on the ocean every which way, round and around, upside down in a storm. I dream of parties in high school, college, my childhood home—they are all the same party. Then I am just in NYC with strangely dressed people.

A small child is missing. No one wants to check the basement because it is scary down there. My cats had wandered down there, and I assure everyone that's where the small child is, still alive.

I dream that my best friend is moving into an apartment deep in the bowels of this building (not the basement, thank God). It has no windows, and to move her in we have to install carpets on the walls and floor to hide the tubing and insulation.

Simon is there, and he sees me. I keep trying to speak to Simon alone. I have to tell him he's in danger. I can't.

And Sarah—who I am not and yet still am—is a lost cause, I know. Still, she refuses to die.

Simon wants to die. Two twins on either breast, neither exist but both of them drain. Coincidences. Dreams. Data processing. Number crunching. Seemingly insignificant discrepancies can blossom and bloom into turbulent, unpredictable pictures.

I dream I'm in a music video for this Portishead song with the chorus, "*How does it feel—this moment?*" I am lying on something like a gurney. I am supposed to be a dead body.

A model, who is in the video, is wheeling the gurney, moving her lips to the music. As I try to get up and off the gurney, she moves toward the huge leather straps as if my resistance were part of the video, part of the song, to show my refusal to be dead, even though I still am dead.

I start wheeling the thing, pushing and pulling away from her, and suddenly I'm in the downstairs hallway of my childhood home, moving my arms in a back butterfly stroke and moving like I'm in the water and the gurney is rushing away from the model. The hallway is dark and the wraith (my mind confusing the words wraith and waif because I think that 'wraith' is commonly used to describe models) is chasing me, screaming in frustration.

I know there is a door at the end of the hallway that leads outside.

My room, which has a door with a lock, is the last door on the far right wall. I time my jump off the gurney with the sound of the gurney hitting the back door. I escape into my room and close the door, turning the little knob to lock it just as the wraiths' hands touch it from the outside.

The music changes immediately to Ella Fitzgerald who is singing "I'd rather be lonesome than happy with somebody else."

I awake, motionless with the terror of the lingering image of flying backwards as the wraith screamed and chased me.

I had broken a contract. I was supposed to be dead, or at least *act* dead.

A CHEAP SANDWICH

YOU AWAKE ON THE COUCH with your hand asleep. The palm tingles. You remember that you are you, after all, and feel somewhat angry, cheated by the dream and your Jeep and that dread-locked dude and your neighbor, Bill, like they have all conspired to confuse you in some way you can't put your finger on. You are quickly on your feet, regretting your decision to call in sick, regretting the getting of this stupid couch, which you kick in anger.

You stub your toe on that kick so badly you think you've sprained it, and you hop around the room singing "ow-ow-ow."

"*Doooon't,*" sings a clear soprano voice, "*let it get...*" Beautiful — but distant. Is it coming from across the alley? One of your neighbors, no doubt, also playing hooky from work. "*...you so upset, my dear.*"

You take your guitar from its case and begin strumming in the same key as the voice, which does not continue. "*Don't let it get you so upset, baby,"* you sing, in your low, lusty voice. *"Don't let it get you down."*

You play your guitar for two hours, until your fingers are sore, and you have a new song to show for it. You think it's pretty good but you need to try it out on someone.

Your belly is talking, asking for something to eat, and you leave your apartment to get a sandwich and check on the status of your Jeep.

It was gray this morning, but now the day is a smoked-sunny.

Your Jeep is ready, a new alternator and a new battery and a hefty six hundred dollar bill. You put it on your credit card (you have excellent, carte blanche credit) and drive your Jeep, both of you humming happily, to a sandwich shop.

A foot-long meatball sub to-go, reminds you well enough that you are still a man's man, a meat man, a music-making man. You flirt with the girl making your sandwich. She looks about eighteen, she wears blue eye-shadow and an adorable smile.

"How are you today, Tricia?" you ask the girl, Tricia, according to her nametag.

"Just fine," she says.

"My name's Rich."

"Hey, Rich," she says, blandly.

"I'm a musician," you say. "I just wrote a new song."

"Cool," she says.

"Do you want to hear it?" you ask.

She doesn't answer.

"When do you get off?"

"Whenever I can, baby," she says, running her tongue over her lips with a wink. Then she gives a huge laugh, and you realize you are the joke. "Just kidding," she says, looking over her shoulder for her manager, you guess. "Look, I have a boyfriend. Do you want the value meal with that?"

You don't want the value meal, you feel embarrassed to death in front of... well, that guy sitting over there minding his own business.

You pay for your sandwich without looking her in the eye. Tricia is feeling sorry for you; you can tell because she says, in a whisper, "Hey, I'm really sorry. I didn't mean to be rude. I think you're cute, but I do have a boyfriend."

"Hey, it's okay," you say, playing up your hurt-card. "I just wrote a new song. I just wanted someone to hear it. I'm new here." She's not even that cute, you know.

"I can tell," she says, smiling, still making fun, but there's no bite. She hands you your change. "I get off work at six," she says. "My boyfriend's working tonight, so... I don't mind hearing your new song, if you wanna come back."

"Okay," you say, toying with standing her up now that she clearly wants you. "I'll be here at six."

So what do you do?

Do you drive home, eat your meatball sub,
and make sure you are watching Must See Shit-coms
between 5:30 and 6:30?

—*Or*—

> *Do you endeavor to show Tricia, who showed*
> *you a little pity, a little respect by showing up*
> *when you said you would?*

What sort of guy are you?

This kind, I hope:

At five fifty-five, you sit in your Jeep in the sandwich shop parking lot, watching Tricia through the large windows as she wipes the glass casings with a rag. You don't want to walk in until precisely six o'clock. You don't want her to think you're desperate. Besides, you feel so tender, seeing her like this — from the outside.

You feel a sort of strange pride in her, at the way she talks to the pimply boy over her shoulder. You feel something like love at the way she puts her hand on her hip and throws her head back to laugh. You start to sing to yourself, watching her, the lyrics you wrote today. How did they go?

"Don't get too upset, baby. Love does not forget, baby. And you can surely bet, we sing a strange duet..." Where did those lyrics come from, you wonder? Where inside you was that song? Did it come from a dream? No, you just sat there, on your couch, and played... music.

You get out of your Jeep, stretching your legs. You've been sitting in the parking lot for well over twenty minutes. You look at your watch. 6:03. Oh well, here goes. The pimply boy regards you with a leer as you enter, but Tricia has a warm smile for your pains that tugs something inside and triggers the desire to start singing right here, right now.

You don't.

She takes your arm as you walk across the parking lot.

"You're cuter than I remembered," she says to you.

"Really?" you say, pulling your lips in, an unconscious facial twitch? A gesture you don't know you have that Tricia finds thankfully charming.

You get a six-pack of light beer on the way back to your place.

When you get to your apartment, she rhapsodizes for ten minutes about how much she loves the couch, then surprises you by jumping your bones on it immediately.

After you've done it, you say, "I thought you had a boyfriend."

"Well, it's not like I'm married or anything."

"I can probably take him," you say.

"Probably," she says. "He's short. And a pacifist."

You strap on your guitar and play your song for her. Your voice conveys something deep and urgent. Your guitar meets it and carries it until you have stopped because you have said all you wanted to say. This is, my friend, the best you have ever performed. You feel it. Yes. It is good you have come here to L.A. It is good you have followed your dream. It is a good song, and it is right. It is rock and roll.

Tricia is applauding furiously, saying "Oh my God! Oh, my, God! That was so amazing!"

Just then, the lights in your apartment die for a moment, only to be reborn immediately, like electric applause.

You spend the rest of the night with Tricia from the sandwich shop. You drink light beer and you tell her about your home in Missouri.

You tell her how your dog died when you were a kid, and your eyes fill with tears. You lie together on the couch, and she gives you a killer hummer. You play guitar for her again and again and again, every song she can think of, every song you can sing.

STANDING UP
ON YOUR COUCH

JUST KIDDING. YOU AREN'T *THAT* COOL. You're too much of a dumbass to be grateful for such kindness shown in a sandwich shop. Rather, you take the opportunity to have some queer petty revenge on the girl by standing her up and watching shit-coms, just to prove that you have the power to be socially cruel, too.

At around 6:00 p.m. you eat the other half of your meatball sub and watch a *Full House* re-run. You are surprised to hear a knock at your door. Thinking it must be your downstairs neighbor, who makes it up the stairs about once a week to bitch that your water is on and leaking into her apartment (ludicrous), you open the door without asking who it is.

A tall, dark and handsome man stands just outside your door-frame. He is about 6'3", with large brown eyes, perfectly shaped pink lips, fashionable facial growth and a fancy gray suit. He looks like a model. Or a movie star. You feel like an ass in your mangy polo with a meatball in your mouth, but then again, he's at your door so fuck him.

"Yeah?" you say, trying to swallow.

He has a legal pad in his hand and a small Dictaphone. He extends a hand towards you, and you take it with your left palm, the one without a sandwich.

His shake is firm, his skin dry and smooth, his touch electric. In fact, you get a little shock from it, like he's been walking on a shag carpet in bare feet.

"Mr. Jamison?"

"Yes?" you swallow. "How'd you get in past the front gate?"

"Sorry, the nice lady, uh — Ethel, let me in. My name is Simon Would, I was wondering if I might have a moment of your time."

You don't invite him in. He's probably a proselytizer here to tell you about the after-life (Ironically, both false and true).

"I am a journalist, and I'm writing a piece about the person who occupied this apartment before you. Are you familiar with any of the circumstances surrounding the previous tenant?"

"No," you say. "What sort of journalist are you? What did you say your name was?"

"Simon Would."

"I've heard of you."

"Yes, I write for major publications — published a book about the sex scandal of Senator Whosishummin some years back."

"Oh. So this is some big deal story you're working on."

He smiles. He is drop-dead gorgeous. Not that you are attracted to men, but you are forced to call a spade a spade. He should be a movie star. "I like to think of it as a human interest piece. I am building a book around it, though."

"So...," you struggle for something to say that will show you are intelligent. "What was it with this guy that was so—you know—make you wanna write a book about him?"

"It was a woman. She killed herself in this apartment, they speculate, about a year ago."

"Uh-huh." You didn't know that someone offed themselves in your place. Yuck.

"Nice girl, pretty girl. Party girl. Worked as an assistant and secretary off and on. An aspiring singer."

You clear your throat and affect a good-ole boy look at him. "So what's the angle? I mean, I know a thing or two about writing and pardon my—whatever the word is—but people commit suicide all the time and no famous journalist gets all up in arms about it."

"Right. Well, you could say I have some personal interest."

You nod like you know what this means.

"May I come in?"

You guess so. He seems safe enough. He is wearing a very nice suit and he is extremely good-looking. You are rather in awe of his manly presence.

He steps into your apartment, taking in the walls, the carpet, the couch. He jots something down on his legal pad.

"What did you write?" you ask.

He looks at the paper, like he's just forgotten he wrote something. "Beige," he reads.

See, that is strange because your carpet is light blue and the walls are white and the couch is blue. *Nothing* is beige. Maybe he's color-blind.

He looks at the couch, actually walks over and touches it, running his fingers along the arm.

"Would you like to sit down?" you ask.

"May I stand?" he replies, as if offended by the suggestion.

You want to protest that you only asked him if he wanted to sit because he was practically molesting your couch, but whatever.

"Sure," you say. He did make the couch look appealing. "Mind if I sit?"

"Not at all," he says.

You turn off the television. "I was just watching a little *Full House*, here."

"I am sorry to interrupt that," he says. He is inscrutable.

"Would you like something to drink? I have water and light beer."

"That is very hospitable, Mr. Jamison, but no thank you. I was wondering if you wouldn't mind if I tape-recorded our conversation."

"What kind of conversation are we going to have?"

"I am going to ask you some questions about your apartment." He begins his interrogation.

You shift on the couch, your answers flying out of your mouth before you have a chance to think them over. It is like you have been charmed, hypnotized and you are saying things you hadn't meant to say, answering questions you didn't know you knew the answers to, words coming out of his mouth like small invitations you want to accept with long run-on sentences.

"Electrical issues?" he asks.

"Uh, like, you mean...?" you don't want to disappoint him.

"Lights going off and on?" he clarifies.

"Uh, yeah, definitely."

"Without you touching the switch?"

"Uh, I don't think so. Nothing that I've noticed."

"Leaking?"

"I haven't noticed any leaking but the lady downstairs..."

"Ethel?"

"Yes, Ethel. She's always complaining that water is dripping from my apartment into hers, which is crazy, because there is nothing dripping up here."

"Singing?"

For some reason, this rattles you. "Hey, is this about the condition of the apartment or this girl who died? I mean, why don't you ask if I get her mail?"

"Do you get her mail?"

"Sometimes."

"Addressed to...?"

"Some girl. Sarah."

"Earlier you referred to the previous occupant as a 'he.'"

"What?"

"Earlier you said, 'him,' when I said 'previous occupant.'"

"I didn't say that, I don't think."

"Right, well I wasn't recording so it doesn't really matter. So, you did know that the previous occupant was a girl and that her name was Sarah?"

"Well, I know that somebody gets mail at this address named Sarah, so, yeah."

"What sort of mail?"

"Junk mail, I guess. Weird church newsletters, um... typical sweepstakes stuff."

"What do you do with the mail?"

"Write 'Return to Sender' or throw it away, I guess."

"You know, tampering with someone's mail is a federal offense."

And suddenly you feel like you have let a snake coil around you, and you are about to be squeezed. "It was junk mail, just trash. I wasn't tampering, I swear."

Simon smiles like a snake. "I was just kidding."

"You didn't sound like you were kidding," you return, a bit frightened.

"It's one of my problems, Mr. Jamison. Sarcasm is often confusing. The French don't get it at all."

"The French?"

"You ever been to France?"

You are in danger. You know it now. This Simon character is not to be trusted. You need to get him out, but you have to be careful. "Look, um, can I get back to watching television and eating my sandwich, please?"

"Sure. Of course." Simon walks over to the Dictaphone and picks it up off the couch. He does not switch it off, though, you notice. It is still recording. What have you agreed to? What have you said? "Are you going to tell me what this is all about?" you ask, feeling a little violated and unsure what has just happened to you.

"Hm?" Simon says, staring at the little red light on the machine.

"The girl. Why the big story? Why the questions?"

"Oh, I wanted to let you get back to your sandwich and this delightful show," Simon says, without a trace of anything but sincerity.

"No, tell me," you insist. "I want to know. What's the big deal?"

Simon looks you in the eye and you swallow, with difficulty, under his gaze. You feel confused in about seventeen different ways you can't even imagine right now.

"I'm investigating the possibility of your apartment being haunted, Mr. Jamison."

You let out a guffaw. Now he is joking. But he doesn't smile. "You're kidding," you say. He meets your gaze but does not dignify it with a response. He is clearly not joking. "I thought you were a serious journalist."

"Well, I'm not responsible for your expectations, Mr. Jamison. Good evening." Simon walks toward your door and you feel like a holiday, one of the fun ones, is about to be over. He can't just leave. You must stop him!

"Hey, how did she kill herself?" you call after him.

Simon turns around, his eyes blank, his face blank. He may be telling you the weather report or the traffic on the 405. "Slit her wrists, suffocated, drowned in the bathtub."

He is shitting you. "Which one?" you ask.

"She slit her wrists in the shape of two crosses—here and here." He indicates with a gesture of the Dictaphone against his wrist. "She did this, apparently, in her bed, and then moved to the bath-tub where she suffocated, somehow, before she drowned or bled to death."

You can think of no suitable response.

"God... Whoa."

"Indeed. Yes, the trail of blood on the carpet from the bed to the bathroom seemed to indicate that she was carried."

There is something frightening in his eyes, something wrong in the way his voice says these words. Is he lying? Is he suspicious? Just who is this man and why do you suddenly feel prickly chills, not at his story but at his voice, his manner, his black eyes?

"Whoa," you say trying to swallow, unable to break eye-contact.

"Yet no signs of entry or exit into the apartment. No sign of any sort of trouble inside. She was well liked, didn't seem depressed, had no enemies, and she certainly wasn't religious." He is a charmer, a snake of some sort, and he is going to swallow you whole in one moment. But first he will strike—do not alarm him, do not let him know that you know.

"Hmm," you say.

"Hmm." He agrees.

"It's funny then," you say, not finding it funny at all. "all the church newsletters."

"Indeed," he says, and gives you a rewarding slight up-turn of his lips. He looks elsewhere, and then back again, his eyes warm milk chocolate dark and sweet. "I don't suppose you saved any of them."

"No," you say, "I'm sorry." You are sorry you didn't save them. Oh, you would love to give them to him.

"Well, again, thank you for your time, Mr. Jamison, and please let me give you my card in case any more mail comes or anything does go bump in the night."

"You mean if someone starts rattling around my bed in chains?" you ask.

What were you thinking earlier? This guy is so awesome. This guy is someone you can really admire, look up to, everything about him is so cool.

"Something like that."

"You're not going to start playing spooky music through the roof now, to get a story, are you?" you ask, feeling like a numb-nuts as soon as it comes out of your mouth. You're just trying to joke with him, let him know you're a guy's guy, someone to have a drink with, someone he should high-five.

Simon continues to smile, but it is a smile he would give a toddler. He hands you his card. He does not answer your question, only turns off the recorder and places it in his pocket. He walks towards the door. "I'll show myself out."

Suddenly you cannot imagine him leaving, cannot imagine how you could possibly let him go. There is something so magnetic in him, so charismatic that you are kicking yourself for being such an ass—you could have provided more detailed answers to his questions. You jump up, running to open the door for him, trying to be polite.

"I'm sorry I couldn't be more help, Mr. Would. Good luck on your story. I will call you if anything comes up."

"Wonderful."

"You do seem like a very serious reporter," you say, trying to find the least transparent form of flattery. You do not think complimenting his looks would look good on you.

"Thank you." He is barely listening to you.

"And I know you must care a lot about writing a good story."

"The girl," he says. His eyes are back on yours, locked.

"What?"

"I care a lot about the girl."

"But...," The confusion grapples you again, and you are at a loss. "She's dead, right?"

He smiles. "What is 'dead,' really?"

DEAD LETTERS

YOUR HEAD IS AT A STRANGE ANGLE as you lie on your couch, staring at the gray business card with black embossed letters. "Simon Would," it says, and then it lists a number for him with the area code "310." Your area code. Maybe he lives close by.

No title. No profession. People just know who he is, you suppose. Not like you, you don't even have your new business cards for Brighton Research. You should yell at... somebody... to get those for you.

What if Simon needed to contact you? He could find you here, as he's done before. But what if you had left this evening? What if you had gone to the sandwich shop and he had come by and not found you here, not told you what horrors had occurred in your apartment, not touched your couch where your head now rests?

But then again, you wouldn't want to give him a business card for Brighton since you are a musician, not a tool. Why didn't you play him your new song? Why didn't he ask about the guitar? I mean, just look at it—out and about like it's dressed up for town. Why didn't you bring it up? What's wrong with you?

And the card slips from your hand and down the dark canyon between the arm rest and the seat cushion. Cursing, you push your hand down to find it, but it has fallen down the rabbit hole, so to speak, and you must remove the cushions to get it back.

The business card has nestled in between three envelopes, stuck deep between the hide-a-bed (that's why the couch is so heavy, after all) and the armrest, being held in place by several springs.

You have to remove the envelopes to get the business card, but they all come free with a minor tug. All envelopes are addressed with a name only, no numbers, no return address. All sealed.

You feel around for any other items in the couch, but other than dust, you've got what there is for the getting. You put the seat cushion back and sit on the couch, fanning out the papers like a hand in poker. Here's what you've got: one gray business card, three white envelopes. All say the same thing: "Simon Would."

Only one has any contact information, the smallest and grayest. Now, it appears that you must decide how to play your hand. Because even though you don't know what game you're playing, you know you have some killer cards. Unsure of what to do, you decide to just hold 'em.

HOLDING YOUR HAND

YOUR DAY AT WORK IS BENEATH MENTIONING. Everything good happens when you get home. First thing, your apartment is unbelievably warm and humming when you enter. Lights are on you didn't leave on. There is a scent of smoke from a cigarette, which you hunt for and cannot find.

The letters, which you placed in your drawer in your bedroom, are prominently displayed in the center of the living room floor in a cross shape with the gray business card—which you had placed in your wallet—in the center, all names up.

Nothing else is disturbed.

This freaks you out so badly that you almost call the cops to say there was an intruder, but do not for fear of the stupidity of your story. After all, they are not letters to you. What else would you say, "someone broke into my house and turned on my lights and smoked a cigarette! I'm sure of it!" Crazy.

It's funny. You have all the cold energy that makes this place seem like a tomb. It's me that breathes life into this place, even from beyond the grave. It is, after all, my place. I was here first and second and always. It is not as if you have ever been, in the slightest way, accommodating or friendly. It is not as if you have any comprehension of who I am or who I was. Your congested, claustrophobic cube of a mind needs some widening, but you refuse to open without some sort of explosion. You continue thinking we are so different because I am dead and you are living. You will find out soon enough.

Sad, really—you. Sad. Me—happy. Well, not happy exactly but okay, fine, all right when all is said and done despite the fact that I am a fucking pissed off spirit because my poor pretty body came to an inexplicable bad end. Despite that, well, I'm still learning and growing, here, without a mechanism to learn or grow. For example, I just learned how to smoke from past the veil. I have to keep it quiet, though, because otherwise all these jonesing spirits are going to come begging me to teach them. Most spirits have to go through the trouble of being born to a new set of lungs so they can start smoking again. Me, I have a special skill. I'm trying to get better so I can do it while you're around.

You pick up the letters, hands shaking. They are still sealed. Your mind darts about its four walls searching for logical explanations.

You come up with:

1.) You are getting older and somehow forgot you placed the letters here in the shape of the cross on which Our Lord died for our sins. The smell of smoke is your imagination.

2.) Someone is watching you and fucking with you.

3.) A ghost is that someone (uh—hello? Duh). Whether or not you believe in ghosts you are still afraid of them so you go straight to the fastest, most anonymous source of information, the truest smack on the street, the world wide web.

There are many support groups for the ghost-visited that you find, though you are not fully prepared to admit you are so afflicted. (Christ, you keep looking over your shoulder, looking for me. I'm right here — reading what you're reading — I don't need to read over your shoulder).

Madame Azura, the psychic/telekinetic healer, offers the following advice:

IMPORTANT TIPS FOR THE HAUNTED:

Ghosts have no physical presence, therefore anything you see or feel vis-a-vis their physical presence is an interactive creation between YOUR physical state and their rut. They are not REALLY there — it is an iteration continuing to its logical end and has nothing to do with you.

You can live with a ghost if you are prepared to be creative. Often they have very simple objectives that they need performed but cannot perform as they are "no longer with us." It is a terrible conundrum for them to be in and often results in the characteristic wailing, knocking, and spooking.

Putting flowers on their grave, moving a piece of furniture, saying a blessing on the house is often all that is required to discontinue the tantrums and to settle into what is easily mistaken for the house "settling." Often the spirits will be grateful and will reward the living body with dog-like devotion.

Sometimes, the objective is not so easily accomplished or the living being will not wish to accomplish it, as in, "Get Out!" Ghosts are often protective of their spaces and do not like the distraction of the living. In such instances, it helps to remember the following in making your decision:

Ghosts cannot hurt you. They can scare you, they can fill you with cold chills, they can make your heart pound, they can momentarily paralyze you when they enter a room. But these physical sensations are due to the living's inability to accept the non-physical presence and the instinctual fear of the dead. Once you have overcome this fear, a ghost is powerless.

A ghost cannot hurt you, but do beware: Ghosts can feed off the living's energy and become more powerful from the living's fear and pain. Other types of ghosts can feed off the living's love or ambition. In certain rare cases, a relationship between the living and the dead develops where the dead feeds off the living, and the living feeds off the dead.

These are the most dangerous instances, for the living person is like a ghost and the ghost is like a living person and the differences between them blur. Such powerful cross-feedings cannot help but breed mis-

fortune and malevolence. The ghost cannot properly continue its spiritual journey to a new body or new beginning, and the living exists in a state of death. Most ghosts understand this, most living understand this, and they respect each other's space and journey.

It is an extremely rare instance where a loss is so great or a fascination is so sick that a living being decides to enter the realm of the dead. Ghosts cannot hurt you, but you can hurt yourself. Beware your own demons when dealing with the spirits.

BACK TO HOLDING
YOUR HAND

THE WHISTLES AND BELLS GO OFF IN YOUR HEAD loud enough
for me to hear. You think of that handsome Simon Would and the
way he said, "I care a lot about the girl." And what about his closing
creepy query, "What is dead, really?"

You know what 'dead' is really, no pulse!

You don't want to touch the envelopes, but you sure as shit want
them out of your apartment, right now. God, look at you! Wringing
your hands and pacing circles around the paper cross.

If I had any idea it would be this effective...

Calm down! Listen. This is all very innocent, really. You're
just bent out of shape because of the misinformation you received
online. I know all the Grade A, top-knotch psychics, and believe
you me, none of them are anything like Madame Azura. Or Edna

Hobokoppin. That's Madame Azura's given name. No lie.

She is a short, squat, pale pudding face with dazed eyes. She makes a living giving $.02 advice about love, money and careers for $2.00 a minute. She has worked her way up from a phone psychic who sometimes had to double on the sex lines when it was slow or one of the other girls couldn't come in. She made a name for herself by branching off into contact with the dead; the money and prestige in channeling and exorcism far exceeds that in telling the desperate their futures.

Madame Azura is not a good witch or a bad witch. She's not a witch at all, just old and ugly. Her powers are as impressive as a piece of toast. To the spiritually starving, this is impressive, indeed. I'm telling you this about Edna because you were so taken with her advice, which is, quite frankly, shit.

She doesn't know a thing about cooperation with the spirits. The reason she can, on occasion, get a voice on the line from the other side is that she is like a fucking annoying tele-marketer who has a sixth sense about when you are waiting for someone really good to call. Once she gets you one the line, well, that's more than most people ever get so they're psyched. She doesn't know a thing about hauntings, but her energy is so repellant to the spirits, they usually try and keep away from her.

She's absolutely no fun. She's never partied in her life and never will in death, either. She's a terrible clinger. Once she gets ahold of a spirit, she whacks it around like your worst, meanest, stupidest teacher.

She's not a bad person, or anything, just a very new soul and a bottom-feeder. I know Edna, you see, we go way back. I worked for a stint on the phone sex line for $9.00/hr (ouch) and would double for the psychics. Edna was the worst of the lot, which was a pretty trashy lot (including me, at the time—I'll tell you about it later) because she was given to frequent moralizing that would really bum everybody out.

She liked to make customers cry. In this way, she was good at her job because once she had broken them down, they needed her to tell them what to do at $2.00 a minute of which she got a commission on top of $9.00/hr because she was a veteran.

I quit my job after I got my first paycheck and realized I'd be much, much happier slinging actual shit for actual peanuts. Two years later, I'm working at an office and my co-worker gives me a birthday present: a gift certificate (no shit) for a phone consultation with her psychic, Madame Azura. I had my own psychic friends, but you can never have too many, and I never turned down freebies.

Now Madame Azura hadn't been Madame Azura when I worked the phone lines. She'd been Madame Krystal, and I had known her as Edna, so wasn't I surprised when I called the number and realized that my co-worker was a sucker and Edna had been promoted. For a supposed psychic, you think she would recognize my voice (which is at the very least empirically distinctive—YOU recognize it, and you've only known me 'dead'). At the very least, she should've clued in to my name as her old co-worker, but she was either too oblivious, or "professional," to let on any recognition.

First thing she says to me is, "You are hiding from the truth!"

How's that for projection? Are you listening? Who are you calling? *Are you seriously calling that fucking phony psychic Madame Azura just to piss me off? Fine. See if I care.*

What the fuck do you think she's gonna do? Bore me to death? I'm already dead! (See, one of the first things a psychic worth her salt should tell you is there is a BIG difference between ghosts and spirits. Ghosts DON'T KNOW THEY ARE DEAD! Sheesh. I'm a freaking SPIRIT).

Waiting on hold. $3.35 a minute, by the by. ($2.00 was when she worked at the Psychic Hotline, not her OWN hotline). Isn't that hold music funny? Now you know why they call themselves 'Madames.' They run a brothel, of a sort. High-level spirit hookers. Not that I'm one to talk. I mean, I was never a hooker, but I was a slut. I guess I did work the sex line for a week, so I guess I kind of was a hooker — but I'm dead now, so who cares?).

God, Dick. You are just getting raped here. Listen, I'm gonna say your name. "Di-ick."

Yeah, look around. I bet you HATE to be called Dick. Well, I hate to be ignored.

Your radio turns on. Kurt Cobain sings *"Rape Me. Rape me, my friend."*

You can't take it. You drop the phone and go turn off the radio.

I can't take it. You've wasted nine dollars without talking to anyone, that's why I just hung up on you. Yeah, sorry — that's a dial tone you're hearing.

Oh, shit. Don't cry. Come on, now.

I don't like to make anyone cry, especially a boy such as yourself, who is uncomfortable with such emotions. Come on. I'm just...

I'm sorry, Dick. Richard. I'm sorry, I really just got carried away, I suppose.

...Boo?

FOLD 'EM

LOOK AT YOU, CRYING OVER SOME GHOST. Why you should be ashamed of yourself. Be the man you know that you are and see what you have in your hand. Just look at your cards, for Christ's sake.

Lay them on the table.

The teakettle starts to whistle and you hold the letters over the spout. You don't know much about steaming letters open, but how hard can it be?

Your goal is to avoid trouble, but you should know what you have in your hand before you throw it down. You do a reasonable job of getting the glue to unfasten. The paper bubbles and wrinkles, but it should be fine. They were crumpled down in a couch for who knows how long? The thing that seems to make no sense is... well, read them all and see what you think. They are typewritten. In no particular order:

Dear Simon,

I know this won't do either of us a bit of good but I can't find you anymore so I'm sending you a dead letter. Ha ha.

Love,

Sarah

This next letter pooches at the bottom corner where there is a hard bulge in it. (If you are in middle school, feel free to add "that's what she said" to that sentence, for indeed it is true).

Dear Simon,

Don't kill me this time around. Losing your job, your wife and your grip on reality is not really the outcome you are looking for. There is no mystery here but the one you are creating. We are obsessed with each other and so what. I can get over my obsession just fine. You can get over yours, too. You are after all, still here.

Enclosed is a present. It means a lot!

Love,

Sarah

The bulge reveals itself to be a blue wooden bead. Some present!

Dear Simon,

Why are you doing this?

Are you looking for me, for her, for some answer or just for yourself?

How will you bring yourself to justice?

Don't you know that you will never reach the bottom
of this?

Seriously.

Sarah

Now you got something strange in your hands, wet with steam
that makes no sense, boy. Now you don't know what exactly you
got yourself mixed into. Suddenly you start thinking about Ethel
downstairs, and her "weeping" walls.

Now you start thinking about how the lights turn off and on
and that strange sound of a woman singing that comes from inside
your apartment, damn straight.

You know your bed has moved itself and that you had a dream
that awoke you one night, paralyzed, and you were sure something
was in your room.

There's no more denying it. Now you know that you are haunted.

You look out into the air around you, unsure of where I am, but
give it a try.

"Hi, Sarah," you whisper.

There is a brief silence and then your radio goes on.

See, I knew you liked Neil Diamond.

"*Hello, my friend, hello,*" Neil says.

PLAY IT

AND NOW LIKE TWO RUSTY WHEELS TURNING you realize that this couch once belonged to me, and that this couch has suddenly found its way back in.

You re-seal the envelopes the best you can, licking the same place that Sarah (or Simon) licked the glue.

It doesn't quite stick and you oh-so-carefully dot the "v" of the flap with glue and place them under some books to flatten their appearance.

Whatever those letters are, they are definitely something—something for the police, something for Simon, something for you to use against Simon.

You call the number on the business card.

"You have reached the voice-mail of Simon Would. Please leave a message and I will return your call in a timely fashion. If this is an emergency, please page me at..."

What constitutes an 'emergency?' A fire, a bomb threat, Jesus Christ appearing? How about a spirit screaming bloody murder?

Yes, it's a fucking emergency! Just fucking page him so we can get on with this already! Thank you!

You hang up the phone, ready to start crying because I just had a hissy fit and even if you still don't want to believe in me, I know you are still scared of me.

You turn off the radio (which just got very loud a moment ago). Fine. I am sorry I am upsetting you, I just need you to understand.

Listen, (I know you won't, but can't blame a ghost for trying) I need you. I know you are going to fuck it up good, but you are my only option right now. I do not mean to scare you, but you have the psychic intuition of a bar of soap.

I'll sing you a lullaby while we wait for him to call back—would you like that? No, of course you wouldn't.

There's the phone!

Oh, my sweet Simon with his sweetest of all voices—I am going into the phone. Sorry about the little static break-ups.

"Mr. Would?"

"Who's this?" says a snarl on the other side.

"This is Richard Jamison. You came over to my apartment earlier today?"

"Uh-huh?"

"I don't know if this qualifies as an emergency."

"That's okay, Dick."

"Please. Richard, or Rich."

"Okay..."

"I just... there was this couch on the street, and it looked like a nice couch, and I didn't have a couch-"

"I saw the couch. It was a nice couch."

"Right, well, some guy helped me move it upstairs and then today, after you came, your business card fell down the couch, and when I was getting it out I found three letters."

"Okay..."

"And they have your name on them."

Silence.

The phone breaks up a little. You can hear somebody else's conversation. A woman says, "...he's married you know..."

And then you say, "Mr. Would, are you there?"

"I'm on a cell phone. I'm sorry if I'm cutting out. Would you like me to come over there?"

Yes, you would. Yes! Say, yes!

"Can I bring them to you?"

I can't believe you just said that. That's it.

The phone is dead. Dead, Dick. Deader than your apartment's previous occupant. Now what do you want to do?

He's coming here. You wish you had something stronger than light beer, that's for sure. Oh well, drink what you've got.

What do I want to do? That's the real question. I think I want to take a bath. Downstairs, the walls start weeping. You start weeping. What happened here? Where did I go right? Where did I go wrong? What is Simon going to bring with him now—now that it's dark—now that he'll see the letters—now that he'll know that we—I mean he and I, not you...

I'm at a standstill, now.

You are here.

Where am I? Where's my signpost, my blueprint? Simon is coming, and not the Simon I knew, not the Simon who really existed, but this Simon who just cared about a girl. He's not sick, he's not drunk, he's not haunted, he's just fine. You and me, alone and waiting. You're weeping, the walls are weeping and I too, a ghost, am weeping because I don't know why I'm dead but I will as soon as he walks in the door, as soon as he sees the letters, as soon as...

God. What happened to me?

URBAN LEGENDS

SIMON DRIVES OVER TO SARAH'S APARTMENT.

Of course, he should know better. It isn't Sarah's anymore. One should have the proper respect for the living to give them eminence over the dead, especially in habitation.

Simon thinks of several Urban Legends as he drives.

The first, he can't quite remember how it begins, but a high school boy (let's call him Billy) is somehow responsible for his friend's (let's call him Eric) death, but no one knows. Billy is terrified that he will be haunted by dead Eric's ghost, but Billy has heard that if you go to the grave of someone who would haunt you at precisely midnight, and stick a knife in it, the ghost will be punctured as it leaves the grave, rendering it harmless and unable to haunt you.

So Billy, all a-shaking and a-quivering takes his knife to the graveyard a little before midnight (there is something Billy is supposed to say, too, some magic words) and walks over to Eric's grave.

He replays in his head the guilty thing he has done (again, like the magic words, these parts are the McGuffin, a device) and at precisely midnight he sticks the knife in Eric's grave (and says "Bibidee Bobidee Boo!").

Suddenly, Billy is grabbed from below. A hand punctures his chest.

Try as he can, he cannot pull away and his heart is squeezed until he dies.

Next morning, police find Billy at Eric's grave. He had stuck the knife in his own shirt and died of fright.

(Get it? I know—wouldn't the shirt have ripped? But Billy didn't even really pull—he was too chicken shit. This story is relevant to you as you think of burning the letters, burning your entire apartment to get rid of me. You will incinerate yourself in the process, Dick. Believe me, just grow some balls, it'll be cool. Have another Light Beer).

The second Urban Legend Simon considers as he drives is the famous ghost hitchhiker, which is the opposite sort of Urban Legend. The first presumes the supernatural when really there is a logical explanation. This one involves a guy (let's call him Simon) who sees a young lady (Sarah, for kicks) on a foggy evening by the side of the road, desperate for help.

Simon picks up Sarah and drives her to her destination (sometimes Sarah is weeping, sometimes she says nothing, sometimes she smiles sadly).

When Simon arrives at Sarah's destination, she has disappeared from his car. Just like that. Thin air.

Simon soon discovers that Sarah has been dead (for a year to 100 years) and he has driven her ghost which appears (on the anniversary of her death, or just a foggy night) because she died on this road (in a terrible tragedy.) This Urban Legend assumes the ordinary with supernatural revelations. The ghost hitchhiker is relevant to Simon because he thinks he catches glimpses of Sarah from time to time standing behind him in the mirror (he turns, and of course, there is no one), or in the rearview mirror of his car (same), or walking around outside her apartment. (You should know that he circles your place frequently. Since you've arrived he has been spying on you, but has found the voyeurism a yawn.)

Besides thinking of Urban Legends, Simon also thinks of the 200-600 pages in his trunk that he has written on the subject of Sarah While.

He seriously considers taking you, the book, and the letters to a remote location so that the two of your can have a little book burning ritual. Then, when he is asked (by his old friends, his ex-wife, his estranged child, his old employer) how the book is coming along, he will say, in a perfectly even voice, "Oh, I burned it."

At that point, their jaws will slack and their eyes will pop from their heads. It has been years of excuse and justifications how he cannot do such and such and must go hither to do what he must to write this book.

They will inevitably ask the three-letter word that Job asks God: "Why?"

At which point Simon, will say, with his characteristic melt-in-your mouth, melt in your hands, melt in the frozen-Artic-tundra smile: "I burned it because it was dead."

No.

He is not going there.

Instead he stops at a liquor store.

Then he turns around and goes back home.

SEXIST AND TYPIST

LIFE'S NOT REALLY FAIR TO SARAH since she has no choices but dying, being dead, and haunting. Then again, I suppose the same is true about all of us, if you look at it from that perspective, so fuck her.

It is sexist that she's relegated to the breaks or the butcher. The same is true of the poor typewriter. No matter what, it ends up with its head opened, its ribbon pulled every which way so it can be examined in the light. And the typewriter doesn't even have the chance of having some say in its fate.

It is typist, the manner in which it is sacrificed without any sort of pretense of self-determinism. (You are an Electric HP. You take 10-60 ribbon. You never had to think about much because you lived in a box, but then became obsolete. Do your keys stick? If 'A' sticks to 'S' then ass a typewriter, you do not appreciate being treated ass a piece of ass).

And what was this object that was Sarah, this flesh and blood feeling being machine that lived and didn't understand that something or someone created and destroyed and played her?

Do you understand that I was *played*? Used? It isn't about justice, it is about *expression*. What did I get to express? Nothing. Who heard my voice? No one that cared, really.

I didn't get to sing what I needed to sing. I didn't get to do that which I wanted most of all in the world to do. And that's why I'm stuck here, trying to get you to hear.

All the same, all the same, here I am and am not, this ghost of a chance, this not a person who once was this person.

I don't want to resurrect, I just want a voice.

And you and Simon are my only shot, now.

And I hate you both so much for that.

DATE NIGHT

WHERE ARE YOU, RIGHT NOW?

I think perhaps that you are still at work, staring at your computer. I wish your phone would ring and you would answer "hello" in that voice you have — that voice. You would hear no reply because you never knew me, after all, but you still know who I am.

I would say something to you. I considered it. Then decided against it. I was going to tell you that he is doing all my dirty work and what dirty, dirty work it is. Do you know why I decided not to tell you? Do you know why I am going to let you find out on your own? Because I want to see the look on your face.

Priceless. That's why.

Isn't it time for you to go home? Don't you have a play-date scheduled for tonight? He has promised to show you physical, dimensional, reproducible proof that he has *not* just been in his house going slowly (not slowly at all) crazy.

He is going to show you the pages, the proof. You don't want to stay too late or keep him waiting outside. He might just break in, and wait for you inside, in the dark. I know Simon.

I want to call.

I won't call. Just go home, Dick. Just go home.

Your door is open, just a crack. It's dark inside. You had a plan. Do remember what it was? Do you have the bottle of booze? Are you armed?

"Simon?" you call. "Simon are you in there?"

I am sitting inside, in the dark. My place. Your place. His place. I taste your fear and it makes me laugh like the little girl I once was once, a laugh of pure joy. *"Don't throw bouquets at me... don't laugh at my jokes too much, people will say..."* Do you know *Oklahoma!* there in the show-me state? Here's a catchy little ditty, but I've changed it up a little: *"The dead girl and the live boy should be friends..."* It's a catchy little ditty. Please. Come in.

I've said it before, and I'll say it again, like an "I told you so" as plain as the nose on your face: You were never, never alone. You have a ghost.

You hear the drip, drip, drip. Someone is in your bathtub.

Guess who?

Come on, just guess! Is it me? Simon? The Lord Jesus? I can't tell you who—it's a surprise! If I told you, that would spoil it... oh my God, I can barely stand it! I can't wait to see your face when you see...

THE REAL SARAH WHILE
SIGNS HER LETTERS
LIKE THIS

THE REAL SARAH WHILE FEELS LIKE SHIT.

She unexpectedly started menstruating and blood covers her thighs.

She is coming down off acid, hung-over, and sleeping on some-one's floor. She staggers to the bathroom. The bathroom mirror, which she stood in front of last night for what seemed like hours, greets her with an apparition.

Last night she had seemed an angel, a saint, a benevolent vision to the self behind the eyes. Now she sees every pore in various stages of red, angry, flaming. Her eyes swim in broken blood vessels and bottomless pupils. She looks the age of her soul, and she has a very old soul.

She could be terrified, but instead she just tells herself to perk up, it's not so bad. She's only human, after all, and what is born will grow and what is dead will decay. She takes off her clothes and sits in the dirty tub with the stream from the shower hitting her body. She uses the shampoo, the soap with the dubious hairs, the loofah.

Whose house? Whose shower? Whose soap? Images of people pop into her mind but there is no certainty in these figures.

But she is a wanderer and these people are kind to the traveler. She knows that she is welcome without asking.

The key now is to get home. She slips out in the morning hours, leaving the slumber party to the sleeping and a note with flowers and hearts blooming beneath a swirling sun. "Peace! Love! Thanks!" signed, "The Real Sarah While."

DELIVERING THE LETTERS

I'M GOING TO HAVE TO FUCK UP your entire conception of the universe, right now. If you'd made different choices, it would have been over already. Since I fucked you over, feel free to go backwards and find yourself a nice road to a happy ending.

All of the endings are happy compared to what's about to happen to you.

I will present to you one other out, when you are in the thickest, dirtiest, nastiest part. It will all be nothing but a dream, for after all, life is but a... But for now, worlds collide and the ugly truth about the real Simon Would can no longer hide behind the tall gorgeous edifice I created at your apartment earlier this day (Sorry. I'll miss him, too).

And so, the phone rings. You jump, knocking over your light beer (Hilarious to me, as always).

You race to the phone.

It is Simon Would. He sounds, however, quite drunk.

"Listen—whas your name again?" he yells into the phone.

"Richard. Jamison," you say.

"I'm gonna give you my address, Dick. Bring those letters and drive to this address. Comprende? Capiche? You get my drift?"

You write down the address with a shaky hand. Though I have been contemplative since the empty but dripping bathtub (surprise! Ha-ha! Nothing to see here! At least not NOW—but boy, you should have seen the mess a year ago. Whoooooeeee!), you are more than eager to get out of your apartment.

Simon lives in what three years ago was the hippest neighborhood in Los Feliz. Now the hip is on the rapid decline, but it's still a phat pad. (If you think this is nice you should have seen his home sweet home in Beverlywood, when he still had a wife, a kid, and a job.) He affords this luxury on inheritance and credit. He is taking time off to write a book, but he won't let anyone, not anyone, read anything, not anything, until it's done.

It's been a year now since his agent stopped calling. Thank God. Once his editors catch up with him, he may be out on his ass. But he thinks he'll probably blow his brains out before that happens.

He is very close, now, to having enough words to bury Sarah and himself. He already has the hole, and he's close to having enough dirt. But what do you know about that? Nothing.

You are impressed with Simon's place from the outside—impressed, envious and covetous. This will all change the moment you go inside. You ring up from the front gate and no one answers. You ring again. No answer. You are about to go wait by your car when his voice crackles through.

"What the fuck do you want?"

"Simon… this is Richard Jamison."

"So?"

"You told me to come by."

Crackle, crackle. The gate buzzes open.

The hallways are very brightly lit, with mirrors everywhere. You admire.

Number Nine.

The door is opened a crack. You knock and enter. You gasp.

Haunted places are hardly healthy or happy; they're fucking cold and spooky and you want to run away fast screaming. It doesn't matter if you believe in ghosts or not, if you happen to sense one in the room, you will shit yourself. (I am not a ghost, by the way, I am a spirit and there is a big motherfucking difference, bub).

These are the ropes of the human condition. Fear and pain are sore-ridden whores that rape you in the dark before you can say "Jack the Ripper!"

He keeps me here, so I keep him here, grieving and lame and puke-drunk and sick with brain clots and TB and other stuff I'm just waiting to try out on him to see if it takes. He doesn't know what I'm plotting. No one knows my plan. I keep it in a dark hole in a tight box in a far corner where he won't find it until it's too late. I created him, a fucked up, obsessed, haunted, half-baked asshole that someone somewhere is supposed to identify with, but Christ knows he doesn't identify with me. He's terrified of me. That's why he keeps me here this way: Voiceless. He can't hear me.

How terrible is that? You, a dipshit and dumbwit can hear me and this joker keeps me gagged and bound in his attempt to analyze *what?* What he already knows and fears.

He's terrified I'll escape and let out what *really* happened.

In a way, I already have. Simon did come by your house today, but that was not the real Simon Would. That was the Simon Would character I created for another Sarah so it could end pretty.

Wasn't he so beautiful, then? God. I wish it were true.

You, poor baby, still believe it might be and are having a very difficult time adjusting to the shade of Simon now standing before you.

And yeah, also, his place is haunted in a way that your place has never been. Ninety-nine bottles of beer on the wall would be an appropriate theme song for the front room if it were ninety-nine bottles of Jack and they were already empty. But he has one down, and it passes around...

"Drink?"

"No thanks," you say.

"Then I'll take yours," he says, and does.

"You look so... different," you say, as politely as possible.

He looks like shit. You can't get the bronze God that came to your door this afternoon out of your head.

"Spare me, please, the inevitable comparisons to myself. Did you have something for me or are you just here to suck my dick?"

You gingerly open your attaché case and hand over three sealed envelopes. Simon examines them.

"Now," he says, "how the fuck did you get these?"

"Well, it's funny actually," you say, thinking how funny (strange, not ha-ha) that you have already explained this to him "I was looking at your business card and it fell in between the couch cushions and these letters were there. Didn't I tell you on the phone?"

"Honestly, Dick, I don't remember shit."

"Richard, please. Or Rich."

"Did you write these, Dick?"

"I found them, like I told you and please—"

"Just in your couch?"

"Yes, it's quite the coincidence and—"

"Are you shitting me?"

"No, I am not 'shitting' you."

"You say 'shit' like a pussy. Are you a pussy?"

"Uh... no." (Lie! You *do* drink light beer).

"Are you a faggot?"

You are taken aback. You are rarely accused of anything and *never* of being a faggot.

"No," you say, with your most clearly offended facial expression. (But the proof of the pudding is in the tasting, they say).

Simon takes another drink and limps to the kitchen counter where he finds a cigarette.

"Did you fall or something?" you ask.

"Quoi?" asks Simon, lighting his smoke.

You close the door behind you and clear your throat. "You didn't have the limp this morning."

"Are you staying or something?" he asks.

"Well, I..." You are unsatisfied. You demand satisfaction. "You said you didn't know Sarah, but I think that maybe she was your girlfriend."

"Did you say you were gay?" he asks.

"I said I was *not*," you say.

"I am," says Simon, exhaling a beautiful smoke ring. "I'm a faggot, you see, and I don't have 'girlfriends.' Sure, I have girls, who are friends, who let me emote when I need to emote and hook me up with their faggot friends, but that was not the type of girlfriend you meant when you said 'girlfriend'. Right, Dick?"

"Right." You stare at him as he speaks, the way his lips move to form the words and the smoke curling from his mouth. Earlier today, you wanted to be him. Earlier today, he seemed untouchable.

Now, you have a strange pity for him. He seems infinitely touchable.

"Are you leaving now?" he asks.

"No."

You're not. In your eyes, you see Simon both as you first saw him and Simon as he is now, and the two images together form three dimensions that make no sense and at the same time perfect sense. In your head, a music box plays a tune that makes you feel so nostalgic, so sad, so tender, you aren't sure what to do, but you have to steady yourself.

"Tell me," you say, "about Sarah."

Simon sighs deep and sad, moving closer to you. Smoke gets in your eyes, and they become misty.

He has a slight curl to his lips and an evil glint in his eye, but his face is so close to yours, you feel you should kiss him — or punch him.

"I'll make you a deal, Dick. For old time's sake. I'll tell you everything you want to know about Sarah, if you get down on your knees right now and blow me."

For a reason that will always elude you, you take this deal.

As you, Dick, are sucking Simon's dick, the phrase "old times' sake" sticks in your head. You realize that you knew him back in grade school, back when you were both boys, back in the show-me-state.

Yes, you knew him then. And you remember now how you'd taken over the reference room, and Simon scouted the asbestos ceiling for a place to tunnel up. Your job was to research the capabilities of a human body to sustain itself in a head-on collision, for this is how they claimed Simon's mother died. He thought they were just hiding her away from him, as she was too broken to be a proper mother anymore. He thought they were keeping her somewhere at the school. The principal's office, maybe.

You looked at the anatomy book, fascinated by the human body without its skin on. Simon was suddenly distraught about his plans.

"Why would they keep her in the principal's office?" he cried suddenly. "What does *he* have to do with it?"

He came over and sat on your lap and you got a boner. You put his hand on it. He told you to "get back to work" and went back to inspecting the ceiling.

You must have loved him, even then.

And here you are now, swallowing his cum shot, which tastes like whiskey.

You should be proud. You are a prodigy.

Isn't love funny?

Simon has had a lion's share of blow-jobs and you just blew them out of the water. He has to sit down, and gasp for air. Emotion transforms his face and he almost weeps. He fumbles his way to the couch, knocking papers off of it. He is still holding the letters you brought in his hand, however, and has throughout your end of the bargain. They are wet with sweat now, and crumpled. He places them on his chest like a consumptive's Kleenex and breathes like the consumptive who needs that Kleenex.

You are afraid to move, though you have lost all feeling in your legs.

"Okay," he says finally, "What do you want to know about Sarah?"

You try to stand up but its too difficult with the pins and needles in your legs from kneeling. You crawl instead and pull yourself up to sit beside his feet. He needs a cigarette. So do you. Smoking poorly and trying not to cough, you ask, "You came by my place today, why?"

"I don't remember. I don't remember coming by your place. How is this about Sarah?"

"You said you were investigating—you had a tape recorder and—you acted like you thought the place was haunted. I got scared. I thought maybe it was, too."

"You don't think so, anymore."

"No. I'm not even sure someone died there. I think..." you don't want to tell him what you think, but you do anyway. "I think you came by for me."

Simon continues clutching the letters, evidence that your hypothesis is sweet, but wrong.

"Why would I do that? I don't even know who you are."

"Yes you do. Do you remember third grade?! Tunneling up through the ceiling of the reference room!"

"Oh my God, you don't say," says Simon, as if you just reminded him there was a chance of showers tomorrow.

"I didn't remember either. But you said, 'for old times' sake' and I knew you looked familiar—and not just because you'd been on TV."

"You live in Sarah's place."

"I don't know if I believe in Sarah."

"You get her mail, you said."

"You said you don't remember coming by this morning."

"What am I holding in my goddamn hands?" Simon says, sitting up suddenly, holding his fists in front of him.

"You wrote them. You know," you say, bold as brass.

"You read them?"

You ignore the question. "Or she wrote them... or, I'm just saying. Why did you come by today if you don't remember me?"

"I don't remember coming by, and I remember you, now. Yes.

Small world. Thanks for the letters and thanks for the memories that I will wear as a blanket as I drift off to sleep. Now please, fuck off."

"You said you'd tell me about Sarah."

"Now I'm telling you to go home."

You don't want to go home.

"Tell me everything," you say.

"Read the book," he says.

"We had a deal."

"So does my agent."

Simon limps to the bathroom. You hear him retching.

You knock on the door. "Are you all right?"

"Fuck off!"

On the couch, the letters look like free candy.

Do you take the letters back before you leave?

—OR—

Take your raw deal/short stick and fuck off 4-ever?

RAW DEAL, NEW TALENT

YOU DRIVE HOME. When you walk in the door, you, Rich, are overwhelmed with the rich spirit—the warmth—of your abode. Compared to Simon's Haunt, your place seems like Disney's Haunt, which is a pretty sweet ride in the happiest place on Earth. You take out your guitar. You play hard and fast, slow and sad—making love out of nothing at all.

You have loved and lost, given and been taken. Love stinks, love bites, love bleeds. You sing yourself songs that salve your sore sucker's love-sick. You voice is low and dirty, throaty and sexy, and you have found the one thing you lacked: A broken heart.

It will mend by morning. You have also found a new talent: Sucking cock! Ten years from now, you will pick up a college kid hitchhiking and drive him sixty-nine miles to his high school sweetheart's home for Thanksgiving. On the way, you will ask him if he wants you to suck his dick.

"Uh... no," he will say. "That's okay."

"I'm not gay," you will assure him. "I'm just really good at it."

Congratulations! You are a gift to the world: A giver, right to The End.

ICE CREAM, NOT SO NICE DREAM

YOU HAD THAT DREAM AGAIN. But now, here you are, awake, safe, real. You are in your soft bed, a $1,500 double — cushioned King Size contraption with soft white sheets, a soft white comforter, soft white feather pillows.

You turn over onto your stomach. Someone once told you, somewhere, that most dreams are caused by the digesting of food. Merely changing positions will change the dream. Now, you cannot remember the dream. Still, your belly hurts.

What did you have for dinner last night? Pizza apparently can give you funny dreams. Also ice cream. Where did you hear that? It doesn't sound quite reputable. But you did have a small dish of ice cream last night in your kitchen. Vanilla. Nothing like a good vanilla, even after all the thousands of mixing and matching of nuts and fruits and bars of candy with every imaginable flavor under the sun.

You smile at yourself, appreciating that you are strictly a vanilla man, after all, appreciating your morning erection. Yes, good morning. Hello, sun! Hello, tree outside your window! It is a great day to be alive, for you are a wealthy white boy with nothing in the world, nothing in the whole world to give you a lick of trouble.

Good-morning, Kansas City! Good morning, world! You are sixteen again, and you play sports. You have a blonde, popular girl friend who wears pink panties and a C cup.

You get good grades in math and science, without cheating. You have an affable manner that makes you a good boy, and often you hear, "What a nice boy!" "What a charming man he is becoming!" "You must be so proud of him, Shirl."

Shirley is surely proud of her son, yes indeed. You are sixteen—look out the window at the tree, that tree which is your first real memory; that tree in KC, MO, out your window. It has green leaves that look fuzzy and furry, and branches upon branches in every which way that seem to sometimes weep and droop and then lift to the sky.

It is not a climbing tree; it is a looking tree. You lose yourself inside it up and around, its flowing lines like a maze until your eyes become weary and you fall asleep again.

What kind of tree is it? Why do you always forget to ask? Surely Shirley will know the answer. Your Mama knows trees and flowers and roses—and you may fall asleep again, hand on cock, sixteen year old boy with nothing to fear—because it is a Saturday, and you don't have practice till the afternoon and Mama will wake you—and what can be more perfect than you as you are now, looking at this tree, falling back asleep, sixteen, strapping, socially superior, the whole world your birthright, and on top of it all, it is a Saturday.

You will have another dream when you fall back asleep, but like THE END of this one, you will never remember. Sweet dreams.

KNOW WHEN TO WALK AWAY, KNOW WHEN TO RUN

YOU DRIVE HOME, SINGING BITS OF OLD SHOW-TUNES from musicals you never saw. The letters seem to glow through the leather of your case, like they are radioactive gold or kryptonite.

They are precious cargo, now, for better or for worse.

You get back inside your place, shaking your head and laughing at yourself. Why did you do what you did? Can't say, really.

But compared to Simon's place, your place is like a land of pastels and petit-fours. It seems warm and cozy and clean (no thanks to you, bub—I have to light spirit-side Nag Champra, squirt Other Side Holy Water and Next Stage Sage to keep this place from getting that live-person with dead-soul smell. Gnarley).

You sit down to play a little guitar, but you can't play the guitar without a guitar string.

Sorry. I broke them. I tend to break things. You see, while you were gone I was trying to play a little Nirvana of my own and, you know, one thing led to another... anyway, we made beautiful music together—it must have been love, but it's over now.

You actually look around the room like you might see someone there (you are starting to catch on, in your own dim way) and when you see nothing decide to call it a night. I have not had the banner evening you can claim, so I'm rather pissed.

I am not your average friendly ghost, and I come at you like gangbusters as you dream. You don't know the difference between Bo-Diddley and Boo-Radley and every word couched in entendre is lost in the couch. So be it.

We are starting to understand each other, I think. Like any relationship, we need trust and work. I trust that you will fall asleep so I can work on you. You'll get it in the end, you'll see. Open your eyes.

You do.

Sick to your stomach, sticking with sweat, forcing the dream out with the need for a cigarette when you know damn straight you don't smoke. The light goes on. You emit a girlish shriek I find very satisfying.

You can see no one in the room but you. It is cold and you are burning with a fever. You pull on pants and a shirt as quickly as possible, grab your shoes and your wallet, and exit your place locking the door behind you. You pull on your shoes on your way down the steps, causing you to take a nasty spill from which you recover. You walk out into the warm night air and walk to the corner store.

The man who works the counter is outside, smoking. The front doors are locked but he lets you in so you can grab a six pack, a can of Pringles, and a pack of Marlboro Ultra Lights. Simon smokes Reds.

"Late night?" asks the man behind the counter. You ask him to repeat himself since you have trouble understanding anything but Queen's and Red-neck English.

Then you reply, "I—uh—had some trouble sleeping." The man looks at you with dark, knowing eyes. His accent clips.

"Lady trouble?"

"Oh, no." A forced smile on your part. "Just busy, you know. At work."

He nods and you scurry.

On the street, shadows down the block stealth behind corners. Roaches the size of cookies refuse to give you the right of way so you play hopscotch. The outside of your building glows with security lights, creating moving pictures on the white paint with the two front lawn trees. You type in your code at the front security gate and eat Pringles on your way up the steps, the crunch-crunching keeping you focused and reasonable. You search your pockets for your keys. No dice.

You let out a quiet expletive, so as not to disturb the neighbors. You suppose you will have to walk back to the corner store and call a locksmith, make small talk with the man, avoid the roaches and the shadows once again.

It occurs to you that you might be able to break in. It occurs to you that your windows are made up of small horizontal glass slats.

I could give you a choice here, of calling the locksmith or trying to break in, but I put it in your head that you will try to get in first, to make a point.

I am trying to show you something, Dick.

You remove your screen clumsily, cutting your hand on the metal frame. Removing the glass slats is so simple, a four year old could do it. You remove five slats and climb comfortably through to your living room couch. You unlock your front door, go back around, and put it all back together again. A drunk gimp could do it.

Do you get it?

DO I STAY
OR DO I GO NOW?

YOUR VOICE MAIL MESSAGE LIGHT at your Brighton cubicle blips three times. You had just stepped out to pick up a nice Chinese Chicken salad, feeling a little ill from all that you swallowed last night. Three calls. Wow. You enter your password and a murderous voice speaks.

"Listen, you cock-sucker. Listen you two-bit piece of whoring trash. You want me to fuck you up the ass or something?"

'Press one to save this message. Press two to forward this message. Press three to delete this message.'

You press three. Message deleted. How did he get this number? Message two:

"You better be here now, right fucking now with those letters, you ass-wipe." You press three. Message three.

"I'm not playing with you, Dick... Dick, I don't know where you are, but you better be on your way here with those letters, Dick... or I don't know, Dick, what I'm going to do, Dick... to you..."

You press one. You like the sound of his voice in that one. Soft, desperate, defeated. You eat your salad. You put your phone on DND. Let him come into work if he wants you so badly. Let him come to you. You hum through the rest of your day. No more calls, no more messages. You drive home listening to the radio, rocking out to "Bad Moon Rising." He knows where you live.

Who should come to whom?

Maybe he will be there waiting for you when you get home.

No such luck. Inside it is warm and light and I am singing Credence to welcome you home. The letters are in your attaché case, you're sure of this because you've checked on them 73 times today.

I'm not going to touch them. You're doing just fine, Dick. Just fine. Why don't you call Simon over here? Sit tight. Isn't it nice here? I tried extra hard to make the place nice for you today. See?

Look, you gotta help me, man. I am trying hard to understand. I am living in a state of denial where I think I'm still participating in the consummation of love even where I am not physically present. Back and forth between the torments of the flesh and spirit and heaven itself.

It is very confusing. I can't remember when I'm there, why I'm there, and sometimes I just disappear without warning and wind up back in the universal soup with nothing to hang my hat on.

All I know for sure: It has everything to do with how I lost my breath, and a weighty trifle called "love." When I am there, in love, it is as if I am eternally in an adolescent state of life or death though I already know the ending of the story.

I really need your help, man. I ask you because you are sitting on my couch, living in my place and macking on my boyfriend. I ask you because you don't know how I exist and your neurons fire in a perfect square so you will think it is your idea.

It all starts clicking like a game of four-square. Simon lied to you when he first visited. The letters are from Simon to Sarah, and they are what Simon came by looking for. He knew her, all right. Whatever reasons he has for hiding that fact, you don't know. Maybe he would be a suspect.

You saw how easy it was to get into this place.

You remember Simon, standing in this very apartment wearing his nice gray suit saying, "...the trail of blood on the carpet seems to indicate she was carried." And as you used to say in the playground, he who smelt it—dealt it.

A delicious shiver shakes your body.

Simon Would, the murderer! But why? What would be his motive? You need to get a hold of the book he has written.

That will have his entire motive explained as clearly as a blueprint. Steal the pages, if it comes to that ("steal the book" huh? I like the way you're thinking! Good for you!) It's a completely atypical Dick Jamison plot, but sometimes uncharacteristic, naughty things like this happen in our twenties.

Do you question your motives? I don't think you do, since you are putting on cologne and whistling. Wait—you are picking up your keys. Are you going somewhere?

I turn on your favorite radio station. You look back, unalarmed. You should stay.

Do you stay...

—OR—

Do you go, now?

IF I STAY
THERE WILL BE DOUBLE

YOU CALL SIMON'S VOICE-MAIL.

"Simon. This is Richard Jamison. I received those... uh... messages you left today. I thought I'd left the letters, but I... uh... must have taken them with my other stuff when I left. Anyway. I've got them here. You've been here before so, uh... well I just got home, so if you want to come get them, that'd be fine. Also, I'd love to read whatever you've got .,.uh... of your book. So, you know, you could bring that and, that'd be cool. Well, I'll be here, so you can call me back at..."

Sorry about the guitar, Rich. I really didn't mean to break the strings.

You turn on the television. You get a light beer. After two sitcoms, the phone rings.

"Hey, Dick."

"It's Rich, please. And hello, Simon."

"In grade school you were Dick." He does remember you, after all.

"No, I was Rich even then, Simon."

"Hm," he says. "So you accidentally took the letters back? Or you decided fair is fair."

"I don't know. I just have the letters is all, Simon. And if you want to bring the pages you'd written, then I think that would be nice."

"'Nice?'"

"What's fair is fair."

"Exactly. Stand up for yourself, Dick."

"Richard, please."

"Exactly. As soon as I sober up enough to drive, I'll be there."

We are both just so excited! Don't vacuum—what if he rings while you're vacuuming and you can't hear the phone? Go ahead and dust, and use glass cleaner and air freshener and take good stock of your teeth, your breath, and your hair.

I, for my part, am in another dither. Remember when he came the first time? Where was I? Well, I actually stayed in the bedroom with the door shut and sang softly to myself until he left. I was not yet ready for Simon. Maybe I will be now. You see, I had quite the wicked crush on him but then I wound up dead and that was a real drag. Please help me slip into something more comfortable. A sheet, perhaps? No, I'm kidding.

He's here! He is beautiful, isn't he? He walks in, and I start flickering the electricity. Saying hello. I also turn on the stereo.

"Wild is the Wind." Nina Simone. You don't even own the CD. I also start the walls a-weeping. I am going all out for this visit.

If you notice, you don't let on.

"Is this the light flickering you told me about?" says Simon as he enters.

"Oh, I guess," you say.

"You like Nina Simone?" asks Simon.

"Who?"

Simon smirks, and I suppose that's my only applause for my completely exhausting effort. He will have to go to the bathroom to see the weeping walls.

"Letters?" asks Simon.

"Oh, yes." You take them from your attaché case and hand them to Simon, who folds the letters and puts them in his pocket.

"May I smoke in here?" he asks.

You nod. He can do whatever he wants in here. This apartment is his free fly zone, now and forever.

"The pages?" you ask.

"Don't hold me to what I say, Dick. I'm a terrific liar."

You don't know what to say or do, but it doesn't look like Simon is going anywhere soon.

You just stand there looking at him. You are awkward, unsure, and scared of him. It seemed so much easier when you thought about it, but now -

"Where's that music coming from?" asks Simon. The stereo has stopped, but the concert is just beginning.

"What music?" you ask, knowing.

"You don't hear it?"

"What does it sound like?"

"You know," Simon says. You do know. "Like Sarah."

IF I GO
THERE WILL BE TROUBLE

YOU LEAVE THE RADIO ON and lock the door behind you. On your way to Los Feliz, you consider some options.

You got this guy in the family, you see, who's connected in the literary world. You hand him the right combination of words on a sellable amount of paper and you will be a leg up in the artistic world, so to speak.

Not music, exactly, but all paths can use diversionary springboards. The problem is, you write for shit. You know it, I know it, if you had a dog he'd know it, too. Simon Would, on the other hand, writes tried and true tested prose. If you had his shit, and said it was your shit, that would be some sweet smelling selling shit for sho'.

A block ahead of you of you a car makes a left hand turn as an oncoming car races through a red light. The racer slows, then speeds away. You get a clear view of the make and model of the car, even a few letters of the license plate. Nirvana sings "Rape me" on the radio. You keep on driving.

Shaking your keys like they are castanets, you ding Simon's apartment. *"Number Nine"* is not just the most misunderstood Beatles song. It's the most misunderstood apartment in this building.

There's Simon's window, lights off. No answer to your first ring, so you decide upon eight more. He answers number six.

"Hi, Dick," he says.

"Those were some nice messages you left me."

The loud buzz of the gate is his response.

He comes to the door wearing the clothes he wore last night, looking like he hasn't slept, smelling like a pickle.

"Just hand them over," he says. He is so electric. God, you feel it in your knees.

"Now, wait a minute," you say with a salesman's smile, "I thought we had a deal. So, if you don't want to talk about it, I'll give you the letters, and you let me read your book."

"Why do you care about the book?"

"Well, she lived in my apartment. I think I have the right to know. Besides, I care about you." You show two rows of white teeth. "C'mon, for old times' sake."

Simon looks bled by leeches. "Give them back."

You would not, maybe ever, but you break.

You take out the letters and hold them close to your chest, your lip quivering for mercy. "I was just trying to... find out..."

Simon only looks at the letters. "Come on inside," he says, and opens the door wide.

It is so dark inside. So cold. But it is cleaner than it was yester-day. You walk in with an affected jaunt, your neurons firing in their be-bop cadence. "You must have some air-conditioning bill!"

He says nothing, but is staring at your hand which clutches the letters.

"I suppose you make up for it by never turning on the lights," you continue, and laugh at your own wit.

Simon does not. "May I have them, please?"

"Oh, sure," you say, with a gesture like you'd forgotten. "I didn't mean to take them. They just got mixed up with my stuff when I left. Sorry." You're still holding them.

You reach out your hand and he outstretches his. They touch. You hold onto his hand as he takes them from your grasp. Was he not, once, your best friend? Did you not, once, love each other with a love so pure as only to belong to children? Does he not remember? He must remember.

He tears them away, and you watch as he rips them, one by one, into pieces, into the sink where he lights them on fire, burns them to ash, then runs them down the drain and turns on the disposal. When he has finished this focused task, which takes a significant number of minutes, he turns and gives you a bright smile.

"There!" he says.

You smile back.

"How about a drink?" he asks.

"Sure!"

"I even cleaned a glass for you," he hands it to you. He has cleaned a glass—just for you! It's a gift and you know it.

He continues the giving: "I bought beer. You like beer?" he says.

"Of course," you say. "Oh... but I'd like to use the glass."

"You could pour the beer into the glass."

"Great!" He takes a bottle from the fridge (it is even a light beer! See, he knows you!) twists the top, opens your beer, pours it and hands you the full glass and the rest of the bottle.

"Thank you!" you say.

He picks up his bottle of whiskey. He moves it out to clink against your glass.

"To Sarah," he says

"To Sarah," you say. Sipping your light beer you walk over to the coffee table, which is now rather orderly.

On the coffee table there is a typewriter, next to which there is a neatly stacked pile of pages. You move to pick up the first one and Simon immediately slaps your hand and shakes his finger at you.

"No, no," he says.

"Is it finished?" you ask.

He lifts his hands out to the sides in a Christ-like gesture. "It is finished."

"Then why can't I read it?"

"Because then I would have to kill you. You see, I'm going to read it and then kill myself. At least, I would, if I hadn't broken my gun."

"You have a gun?"

He starts to sing (it's Nirvana, so you get it). *"And I swear, that I don't have a gun. No, I don't have a gun."* He gives you a wink.

What does that wink mean? You don't know. You just find that you feel rather sad that he doesn't have a gun, although maybe he is lying and he does, or maybe... it's too confusing.

It makes your head hurt. How are you going to Steal This Book? Is that really what you are here to do, after all?

"Have another drink," Simon says. You do.

"Sit down," Simon says. You do.

"Let's not talk anymore." Simon says.

You close your mouth, following his. You open your mouth

when he opens his. A rough kiss that feels like a call to battle. He is the leader. He pushes your head down onto his groin and closes his eyes and waits. It is a trick. He pulls you off with a force of disgust and walks back to the bottle. He didn't say so, so you lose. It's that same old game from childhood. "Simon Says."

"Let's have another drink," Simon says. You do.

When you come home around midnight, driving drunk, around midnight, you can hear music blaring from the street. There are cops just arriving outside your door. Apparently Ethel called them. The music is coming from your apartment and it is extremely loud. You have to yell to get the cops to hear you.

You insist you did not leave your radio on. They do not believe you. You are lying; you did leave it on.

Sure, I turned it up quite a bit, but fuck you, Dick.

Fuck you.

You play good ole boy with the cops who could give a shit anyway and have murders they aren't looking into to be here dealing with some crazy old lady and your music. They give you a citation. Fuck you.

You don't sleep tonight. You are too busy plotting the basics. Who would have thought you had it in you? Not I, said the dead girl.

First thing you'll do, you think, you'll get him drunk. He's an alcoholic for Christ's sake. You'll just get him to drink and drink and drink until he passes out. Then you'll remove all his clothes and carry him, light as he is, into a warm bath. If he awakes, which he will not, he will thank you for taking such good care of him.

Perhaps you will have to lightly hold his face under the water. You think of his eye opening, closing, lips moving, perhaps just parting—little jewels of oxygen from beneath the water forming on his eyelashes. Maybe he will not wake at all. And then you will get the razor from his bathroom and you will cut his wrists and your hands will be steady and you will slice clean and deep.

It will be a beautiful death for him, like the French Revolutionary (you can't remember his name—but surely Simon knows), and of course, like Sarah. And then you will wait, after separating Simon from his clothes, his flesh from his blood, his breath from his body.

You will wait until that which makes him move and talk and fuck lies spilled out onto the floor.

You will carefully look about for anything that needs to be cleaned. Your shoes, perhaps. In fact, it would be best if you removed all your clothing just in case of blood. You see yourself, naked, with Simon, naked, taking everything he has to give, and a deep peace moves over you. It is a fitting end, you think, for Simon.

Not just because of her (me), not just because he loves her (me), but because he probably killed her (me. You think?). You don't care about that, that he is (you think) a murderer, since you are planning one now, yourself. And whatever motive he had seems like the same motive you have: The pages.

Those pages are his heart. If you steal them, you will have stolen his heart. And isn't that what you really want, really?

If it isn't, this is your last chance.
Just end with the "raw deal and new talent" chapter.

—OR

What is music but the sound of your own heart?
Beating or breaking, your heart must go on.

CROOKED

IN THE SHOWER, YOU REMEMBER part of your dream: You and Simon were making love missionary style on your kitchen table at your home in Kansas City. Your parents could have walked in at any moment. You didn't care. You wanted them to. But you were, in the dream, it is only fair to tell you, not you. You were a woman.

You sit at work, staring at the unblinking red eye of your voice message. You sigh every so often.

On your lunch break, you decide to take a walk. After a few blocks you notice, across the street, a neon sign that says "Madame Azura palms read $10."

Well, golly gee — that could be the same Madame Azura (Edna Hobokoppin) of internet fame!

You have never had your palm read. You don't know which line is which. Who knows — perhaps your cold, clammy meat hook might reveal something.

Maybe something about how you are in love with a man you are about to kill.

Maybe something about how your high school prom date still pines for you. You remember her now only as a prom picture — she strolls about the halls wearing pink lace and a forced, glassy smile. You recall the pleasure in touching her, in getting your rocks off, and it rushes again like proof you are not "gay" but a straight man trapped by a crooked one named Would.

Would you like some advice from Madame Azura?

-OR-

You're too afraid, skeptical, murderous and cheap?

ADVICE

HOLDING ONE PALM WITH THE OTHER HAND'S FINGERS, you walk through a door that tinkles with chimes into a room with cramped head space that smells like incense and piss. Your heart pumps and your palms sweat as you sit on a chintzy couch and stare at kitschy figurines of angels and dragons and crystal rocks.

Madame Azura is a fat white woman with dyed orange hair. She wears a huge pink sari and looks up from a computer where she's been surfing for the last four hours.

She wants money up front and you hand her $10, which she sneers at but takes.

"You need a full consultation — palm, cards, intuitive counseling."

"I only have $10," you say. I don't know whether that's true or not, but that's what you say. She takes your palm in her hand.

"Things not good for you."

"Wait, are we starting already?"

"When you think we start?" She speaks with an accent she must have made up in divination school. On the phone, it sometimes passes for Jamaican if Jamaicans butchered their own dialect and slipped in and out of it at will. You probably don't know the difference.

Do you know enough about Jamaica
to know a fake accent when you hear it?

— *OR* —

What the fuck do you know about Jamaica?
You don't smoke weed and you hate reggae, man.

YOU KNOW NOTHING
ABOUT JAMAICA

"WELL, I'D LIKE TO SIT DOWN, for one thing," you say.

"Back room for sitting. $10 more."

"I've got $5. Will you do it for $5?"

You were lying about only having $10. Madame Azura do not know all, but she certainly knows who has more money than he say.

You hand her the $5, which she sneers at, but walks you through a beaded doorway into a dark room with a card table and two waiting chairs. She takes your hand across the table, lightly touching the pads in your palm, clucking and shaking her head.

"What?" you ask. "What? What? What?"

"You really need full consultation."

"Look, are you trying to rip me off or something?"

Madame Azura drops your hand with a thud onto the card table. "You will not need money anymore, anyway. I try to help someone who is beyond help. You will be dead soon!"

Madame Azura takes credit. $65 dollars later, she is explaining to you that your life-line ends at your heart-line, and you have a line rising from the base of your palm which means soon and sudden death.

"Is there no way this can be avoided?" you shriek.

"There is small branch of possibility... See." She shows you where the sudden death line does have a small hair-like crevice leading away from the head-on collision melee.

"What should I do?" you plead.

"You have been cursed," Madame Azura explains.

"By whom?" you ask.

"An offended spirit."

You immediately think of me, who you don't believe in.

"A girl committed suicide in my house about a year ago." You tell Madame Azura.

"A-ha!" she says. (Oh, God. Now Edna goes in for the kill). She gives you specific instruction how to rid your apartment of "the curse." She, herself, will come and do an exorcism. (Oh, God! Oh, Goody! Maybe she'll figure out it is me! That would really freak her out. But I don't think she will). You do not mention Simon Would. Madame Azura sees nothing.

If you had brought him up, you would have had a different reading indeed. As it is, you are out a total of nearly $3,000 by the end. Having your apartment exorcised is not a cheap operation. ("How much you pay to get rid of roaches? Rats?" asks Madame Azura. "How much worse is offended ghost?"). The exorcism takes hours, and her performance art shakes you to the core with its disturbing display. You will never quite get the smell of sage from your apartment, nor the sight of her squatting and rolling her eyes back in her head while she chanted something awful from your brain. The ghost is gone, but Madame Azura remains.

But in reality, you were never afraid the "ghost" would do you in. Nor were you afraid that some random bus would take your number.

You knew in your heart, head and shaking knees that it would be Simon. Plans, plots and dreams and schemes are quite different from the actual doing. Not only do you not think you are capable of murder, you do not think he is capable of love. And whether or not you mentioned Simon to Madame Azura, it was worth your $3,000 to break with him cold.

In the ensuing weeks after the exorcism, whether walking down the street, sitting at your desk or eating your lunch, you find yourself, palm turned up, staring at the lines. They meet like a malformed wishbone. Sometimes, mid-tuna sandwich, mid-Cobb salad, mid-sentence on the PC, you find yourself in a fatal flash-forward. Your heart will stop, your brain will clot, your throat will seize, an assailant will stab a knife into your back, you will be caught in the cross-fire of a drive-by or you could come home one night and Simon Would will be waiting in the shadows.

So what?

Then nothing, again.

You let out a sigh from your clean, pink lungs and stretch your legs, stretch your arms, check the status of number one.

You are, after all, still Richard Jamison of the Kansas City Jamisons and no palm-reader, no ghost, and no Simon Would can ever change that. Kudos.

In The End, Dick, it's still all about good old #1.

YOU KNOW THAT BITCH
AIN'T FROM JAMAICA

"I THINK WE START AFTER I SIT DOWN," you say, mimicking her accent. She gives you the evil eye.

"Fine," she says. "Sit."

You sit back on the couch and she sits next to you, holding your hand, touching the pads in your palm, clucking, cooing and shaking her head.

"What?" you say. "What? What? What?"

"You really need full consultation."

"Look! That's all the money I have! What kind of rip-off operation is this?"

"Fine!" she says, dropping your hand, which hits your own thigh with a thud and leaves a bruise for you to remember her by. "You are beyond help! You should take all your money, every penny, and give it way to somebody who needs it since you will be dead soon!"

"Oh, please," you say.

"Look for yourself!" she shrieks. "Look at your life-line!"

You calmly turn up your palm. "Which one is my life-line?"

"That one," she says, pointing.

"Well, what of it?"

"You see how it stops at heart-line?"

"Which is the which one now?"

"Here!" she says, pointing to the line that falls like the descent of a sine wave.

"And this one?" You point at the line that begins at the base of your thumb and intersects the sine wave near the base.

"You die soon!" she says, "Not pretty! You better start praying, too! You live a selfish, stupid life."

You laugh. It is not characteristic for you to chuckle at dire forecasts, but with the accent, it is just too obvious. "So," you say. "if I'd given you $50, I'd have a long life of love and financial success, right?"

"Wrong!" she says with a spit. "You insult Madame Azura."

"Listen, Madame Azura, if that is your real name," (I told you it wasn't) you say, "your store is an insult. Your accent is an insult."

"Get out!" she screams. "Get out of my store, dead man!"

You stand up calmly and give her a flourish of your aura's unseen hat.

THINGS GET BROKEN

YOU DON'T NEED ANY ADVICE from a so-called psychic. You don't believe in all that shit. You don't believe in ghosts. You don't believe in anything but you, and you have a plan. You are going to get Simon dead drunk and then dead. Then you are going to steal his book. Yes, it feels right, like it is the only way to... love him.

You are washing dishes, the water so hot it nearly scalds your hands. You are holding a plate and scrubbing and you see, above the sink, beneath where the paint has peeled, words written.

Painted over, maybe once, maybe twice. But you can read them: "Sarah While was here."

And then the crack and the crash and your fingers bleeding.

Things get broken.

You purchase a bottle of whiskey and trip and fall on Simon's stairs on the way to his door. He meets you on the stairs, laughing as the brown liquid breaks the brown bag and glass and liquor leave a trail to his door.

Simon's apartment is clean, tidy, and smells of Nag Champra that burns in an ornate clay holder. His curtains are opened and light spills in.

No bottles. The ash-tray holds less butts than the fingers on your hand.

"Did you hire a maid?" you ask.

Simon laughs casually, like you are a couple of school chums, which of course, you are. "Maybe. You know, the book is done, time to get my shit together."

"Congratulations," you say, not sure you mean it.

"Thank you."

"Sorry I broke the bottle. I don't think we can salvage-"

"Oh, don't worry about it."

"I'll get another."

"Oh, no. It's all right. I'm on the wagon. Isn't that right? On the wagon is when you stop?"

"Yes, I think so." There goes your grand "get him dead drunk" plans. "Do I get to read your book?"

As if he has read all of your thoughts, Simon says, "Of course. It's in my car right now. How about if I bring it over tomorrow? I'll get off the wagon enough to celebrate with you, for old time's sake. For Sarah."

Later, you lie next to Simon in his bed. You are both awake breathing in long luxurious droughts. His hand lays on top of your hand, forgotten. Simon looks at you as if he can actually see you, as if you are actually there.

It is the most exquisite feeling in the world. You cannot stop yourself before you have already said it.

"I love you, Simon."

He smiles. Not the sarcastic, cruel smile he wears most of the time, but a smile from his childhood. "Why."

Not a question. But you answer. "It's just how you make me feel. And, you've been through so much."

"Such as?"

"Well, your mother died. And Sarah. I know you knew Sarah."

"Do you?" He sits up, lights a cigarette, and puts an ashtray between you two. "Do you know that I killed her?"

"I don't believe that," you say. "I know you, Simon."

He hurls the ashtray at the wall. He moves his face in close to yours, his exhale, your inhale.

"You don't know me." Simon says.

"I know you," you protest.

He puts one hand around your throat, the other holds the cigarette.

It is the casualness of his grip that astounds you, and that it is still choking the very life from you. He is killing you now, with one hand. You try to pull his hand off, pull it away, God he's strong he's killing you he's doing it with one hand his grip is so sure and so locked and there's a dark infinity at the end of it and you are helpless. Your eyes roll backwards.

He releases you, and takes a drag. You don't take time to recover.

You are out the door, lucky to be alive.

You drive home, gasping for air and bawling your eyes out, not knowing what will happen next. You can't even play your guitar because you can't play a guitar without a guitar string. You sit on your couch, my couch, and hold yourself in your own embrace, shaking and crying.

I know how you feel, Richard. I walk up the back way to my apartment, backwards. I cannot be much consolation, but I'll sing you a little song. It's called *"Good-bye"* and it's by Night Ranger

He said he was coming tomorrow, bringing his heart with him. It was in his trunk, you see. He'd left it there. Whether or not you let him in, he can get in. Whether or not you can steal his heart, yours is broken.

You can blame him, but in this world, things get broken.

You are lucky it wasn't your neck that was broken. Watch the shadows. You don't know him.

THE BLUE WOODEN BEAD

SARAH'S SECOND RAVE. She took a hit of E in line to get to the door. It was her second time doing E and she thought she knew what to expect, but of course it's hard to know what they cut it with.

She made it through the door to inside where it was like an explosion of Wonderland inside a downtown warehouse. And then, as she got into the throng, she came up so hard that she fell to the floor. She lost her friends in the wave of people and pulled herself to the side of the warehouse as if desperately swimming to shore.

The sensation was like a full-body orgasm, but it was not so much pleasant as just intense and continuing to send her body into spasmodic jerks as she felt everything all at once. Everything too much.

She could feel her mind receding, like it was still in the water and floating away on the Atlantic at night. Her mind was far away.

Just her body remained, on shore, on the hard concrete floor among strangers.

Her fingers found a wooden blue bead that must have fallen off of someone's bracelet or necklace. It was the size of a large olive. It was a boat. It took her body back to her mind, which was getting lost looking up at the stars... but no, there were no stars. She was inside.

"Feel this blue bead beneath your fingers," her body said to her mind. "This is real. You are here."

You are alive.

THE WHITE HAT

THIS HAPPENS AFTER THE MESS including the breaking glass and the cutting of Simon and Simon knowing he is meant to bleed to death in the dark as some atonement that Sarah demands.

Now Simon's conscious-mind comes in like the cavalry.

'Look Simon,' says Simon-mind in the White Hat. 'See here, you aren't going to bleed to death. You sliced your hand and your foot, sure, but it's not like you slit your wrists or anything.'

'Sarah' says Simon, crying in a bloody mess. 'You mean like Sarah'.

'Now, now,' says White Hat Simon. 'I didn't mean to reference old wounds or anything I'm just saying think logically about this, now. This is a bad situation, no doubt, but you will live. Most certainly. In your favor, no major arteries were cut. In your favor, you are sober, my friend! And congratulations on that, by the way. If you were drunk, then we would have a real problem and wouldn't be able to come in and help you. But as it is, you are—we are—going to be just fine. It's nothing supernatural. Never believe your own stories, Simon. You know better than that.'

'Even this story?'

'Stop it now. I'm ignoring that. There's work to do. We need to pick ourselves up and stop the bleeding. Yes, it is dark and there is shattered glass all over the floor. Here is a reminder that you should pay your electrical bill. But let's not get into the I told you so's right now. Right now my sober, non-fatally wounded self, let's stop the bleeding. You need to put pressure on the wound, so let's find ourselves a towel or something. We can easily find something. See. Your eyes are already adjusting to the dark.'

More glass goes into his skin as he tries to find his way, but he barely notices it. He has a mission now. He has to stop the bleeding. His rational mind is here, and that means he is in control.

Sarah and the White Hat cannot be in the same room together.

'Nothing to see here,' says White Hat. 'Nothing to fear. Sarah was never here, after all, Simon, and you know that. Sarah is dead, and has been dead for years.'

White Hat helps Simon shuffle his way around, wrap his wounds. White Hat is a hero. White Hat lets Simon know that what he fears the most is not true, that he is not being punished, he is just being self-absorbed and an alcoholic.

White Hat will come to Simon's rescue always, no matter what, no matter that Simon has a revolver in his closet that he bought for the sheer purpose of shooting the White Hat off his own head forever.

He makes a decision, now.

It is a decision about you.

THE REAPPEARANCE OF
THE MEN IN SUITS

THEY ARE OUTSIDE THE APARTMENT right now.

A STACK OF PROBLEMS

SIMON IS AT YOUR DOOR. In his hands he holds a stack of pages.

"Here," he says. "Take them." He holds them out to you.

It's too late to make a choice about this. You take the pages. Since when could you refuse him? You hold the pages in your hands—a stack about six inches thick of white copy paper, stacked messily as if thrown together in a rush. In no particular order.

Simon immediately is on your couch (it is yours, now, after all), curling up on it, and closing his eyes. Like it was his couch. Like it was the easiest place in the world for him to sleep.

"What do you want me to do with this?" you ask, holding the stack out in front of you, not sure you want to hug it in too close.

Simon looks like he's already out cold but answers: "Read it, please, and let me know what you think."

You think all sorts of things, already. You think you are amazed that Simon said "please." You think you might be insulted by him coming in uninvited, with no reference to how he almost strangled you before, acting like everything is cool between you.

You think that reading the ravings of a madman might be a poor use of your energy. And yet he is so content now, so peaceful, and a happiness—which has been a stranger to these parts as of late—overtakes you.

You sit down with the book. If you read it, and if it's good, who knows, you could very easily just kill him and take it for yourself (it's your apartment after all—and your ghost now). If it's bad, which you wouldn't feel comfortable saying, you'd just play it off all Emperor's New Clothes because YOU never wrote for the *Times* or finished *Ulysses*.

It'll probably get published anyway and you can be its first fan. Regardless of whether you like it or not. Maybe Simon will appreciate the support. Maybe he will listen to you play guitar... maybe you can sing him a song...

"Walk my way... and a thousand violins begin to play." (You didn't hear that. You didn't think it, either).

Maybe his showing you—first!—is an act of faith. Maybe he's saying that he loves you, after all. Who knows what the future holds? You have questions. Maybe in this book, finally, there are answers.

But there aren't.

THE END

IF I WEREN'T A GHOST I would write my story like a house. I would be able to tell you what happened to me, step by step, downstairs to upstairs, touring the spooky attic and basement on either end but landing firmly in the front room where there is light and we know where we are and how we got there.

This and then that, leading us here.

If I weren't dead, too young, too soon, too suspiciously suicidal-looking and no one to really care about it, I would have more power than wind and whispers and weeping walls. Being a ghost comes with certain limitations.

Non-existence is one of them.

That is why you are so important to me, don't you see? You are so vital, so necessary. I have so much I want to tell you, but you are the only voice I have now.

What power have the dead but the living?

What are we dead but your future?

What are you but our past?

And what is time—what is any of this at all—but an electrical storm in the mind, the beat of an organ pumping blood, a dance that goes until it stops without reason, without rhyme, but that which we imagine and create.

Love, too, is a ghost, created through ritual and belief and devotion. Commitment.

Obsession.

Calling back in to itself and recreating what maybe never was, but in the mind of a man…

losing his mind.

THE CHERRY

SIMON IS HUNCHED OVER THE TYPEWRITER, NAKED. Sarah's Santa candle is melting into a horrifying wax figure.

(Candles for wakes and lovers).

Sarah steps out of the darkness into the small pool of light, the sounds of the click-clicking keys awakening her.

"What are you writing?" she asks him.

He looks up at her, cigarette in his lips, as if surprised that she is here at all, at her place. Surprised that she is a real person, here, and not an apparition.

She almost laughs at him. Men look funny naked, especially funny when they are hunched over a keyboard and smoking. She imagines he thinks he looks cool. So she doesn't laugh, but she can't hide the smile playing her mouth.

"What are you writing?" she asks, again. She thinks she loves him. No, she is sure. It is all over now but the crying. She definitely loves him.

"It's about you," he says.

"A love story?" she asks

"A ghost story," he answers.

She stares at him, unsure of what he means. Is it a slap? Is it a joke? Is it… it's something she can't think about right now. Not now. Because she loves him.

"Oh?" she says, taking him at face-value. "But I'm not a ghost."

He shushes her and returns to pecking away at the keys with both hands, like she were interrupting something important. "*Not a ghost*," he mutters her words back to himself, like she said something rude to him and she should have known better.

The smoke from his cigarette is making tears in his eyes and she wishes he would ash it. The red cherry at the end of it looks dangerously close to dropping on his naked lap. That would hurt. And look funny.

It is the moment on the precipice of tragedy or comedy, depending on whether you are the one experiencing or watching.

Is she experiencing, or is she watching? She can't decide.

So she does nothing.

"*Not a ghost?*" his voice rises, indignation cresting at her presumption. "*Who do you think you are?*"

He has a point.

She is nobody.

But it is *her* typewriter, after all.

The cherry drops.

Bizarro books

CATALOG   SPRING 2011

Bizarro Books publishes under the following imprints:

www.rawdogscreamingpress.com

www.eraserheadpress.com

www.afterbirthbooks.com

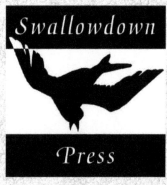

www.swallowdownpress.con

For all your Bizarro needs visit:

WWW.BIZARROCENTRAL.COM

Introduce yourselves to the bizarro fiction genre and all of its authors with the Bizarro Starter Kit series. Each volume features short novels and short stories by ten of the leading bizarro authors, designed to give you a perfect sampling of the genre for only $10.

BB-0X1
"The Bizarro Starter Kit"
(Orange)

Featuring D. Harlan Wilson, Carlton Mellick III, Jeremy Robert Johnson, Kevin L Donihe, Gina Ranalli, Andre Duza, Vincent W. Sakowski, Steve Beard, John Edward Lawson, and Bruce Taylor. **236 pages $10**

BB-0X2
"The Bizarro Starter Kit"
(Blue)

Featuring Ray Fracalossy, Jeremy C. Shipp, Jordan Krall, Mykle Hansen, Andersen Prunty, Eckhard Gerdes, Bradley Sands, Steve Aylett, Christian TeBordo, and Tony Rauch. **244 pages $10**

BB-0X2
"The Bizarro Starter Kit"
(Purple)

Featuring Russell Edson, Athena Villaverde, David Agranoff, Matthew Revert, Andrew Goldfarb, Jeff Burk, Garrett Cook, Kris Saknussemm, Cody Goodfellow, and Cameron Pierce **264 pages $10**

BB-001 **"The Kafka Effekt" D. Harlan Wilson** - A collection of forty-four irreal short stories loosely written in the vein of Franz Kafka, with more than a pinch of William S. Burroughs sprinkled on top. **211 pages $14**

BB-002 **"Satan Burger" Carlton Mellick III** - The cult novel that put Carlton Mellick III on the map ... Six punks get jobs at a fast food restaurant owned by the devil in a city violently overpopulated by surreal alien cultures. **236 pages $14**

BB-003 **"Some Things Are Better Left Unplugged" Vincent Sakwoski** - Join The Man and his Nemesis, the obese tabby, for a nightmare roller coaster ride into this postmodern fantasy. **152 pages $10**

BB-004 **"Shall We Gather At the Garden?" Kevin L Donihe** - Donihe's Debut novel. Midgets take over the world, The Church of Lionel Richie vs. The Church of the Byrds, plant porn and more! **244 pages $14**

BB-005 **"Razor Wire Pubic Hair" Carlton Mellick III** - A genderless humandildo is purchased by a razor dominatrix and brought into her nightmarish world of bizarre sex and mutilation. **176 pages $11**

BB-006 **"Stranger on the Loose" D. Harlan Wilson** - The fiction of Wilson's 2nd collection is planted in the soil of normalcy, but what grows out of that soil is a dark, witty, otherworldly jungle... **228 pages $14**

BB-007 **"The Baby Jesus Butt Plug" Carlton Mellick III** - Using clones of the Baby Jesus for anal sex will be the hip sex fetish of the future. **92 pages $10**

BB-008 **"Fishyfleshed" Carlton Mellick III** - The world of the past is an illogical flatland lacking in dimension and color, a sick-scape of crispy squid people wandering the desert for no apparent reason. **260 pages $14**

BB-009 "Dead Bitch Army" Andre Duza - Step into a world filled with racist teenagers, cannibals, 100 warped Uncle Sams, automobiles with razor-sharp teeth, living graffiti, and a pissed-off zombie bitch out for revenge. **344 pages $16**

BB-010 "The Menstruating Mall" Carlton Mellick III - "The Breakfast Club meets Chopping Mall as directed by David Lynch." - Brian Keene **212 pages $12**

BB-011 "Angel Dust Apocalypse" Jeremy Robert Johnson - Meth-heads, man-made monsters, and murderous Neo-Nazis. "Seriously amazing short stories..." - Chuck Palahniuk, author of Fight Club **184 pages $11**

BB-012 "Ocean of Lard" Kevin L Donihe / Carlton Mellick III - A parody of those old Choose Your Own Adventure kid's books about some very odd pirates sailing on a sea made of animal fat. **176 pages $12**

BB-015 "Foop!" Chris Genoa - Strange happenings are going on at Dactyl, Inc, the world's first and only time travel tourism company.
"A surreal pie in the face!" - Christopher Moore **300 pages $14**

BB-020 "Punk Land" Carlton Mellick III - In the punk version of Heaven, the anarchist utopia is threatened by corporate fascism and only Goblin, Mortician's sperm, and a blue-mohawked female assassin named Shark Girl can stop them. **284 pages $15**

BB-021 "Pseudo-City" D. Harlan Wilson - Pseudo-City exposes what waits in the bathroom stall, under the manhole cover and in the corporate boardroom, all in a way that can only be described as mind-bogglingly irreal. **220 pages $16**

BB-023 "Sex and Death In Television Town" Carlton Mellick III - In the old west, a gang of hermaphrodite gunslingers take refuge from a demon plague in Telos: a town where its citizens have televisions instead of heads. **184 pages $12**

BB-027 **"Siren Promised" Jeremy Robert Johnson & Alan M Clark**
- Nominated for the Bram Stoker Award. A potent mix of bad drugs, bad dreams, brutal bad guys, and surreal/incredible art by Alan M. Clark. **190 pages $13**

BB-030 **"Grape City" Kevin L. Donihe** - More Donihe-style comedic bizarro about a demon named Charles who is forced to work a minimum wage job on Earth after Hell goes out of business. **108 pages $10**

BB-031**"Sea of the Patchwork Cats" Carlton Mellick III** - A quiet dreamlike tale set in the ashes of the human race. For Mellick enthusiasts who also adore The Twilight Zone. **112 pages $10**

BB-032 **"Extinction Journals" Jeremy Robert Johnson** - An uncanny voyage across a newly nuclear America where one man must confront the problems associated with loneliness, insane dieties, radiation, love, and an ever-evolving cockroach suit with a mind of its own. **104 pages $10**

BB-034 **"The Greatest Fucking Moment in Sports" Kevin L. Donihe**
- In the tradition of the surreal anti-sitcom Get A Life comes a tale of triumph and agape love from the master of comedic bizarro. **108 pages $10**

BB-035 **"The Troublesome Amputee" John Edward Lawson** - Disturbing verse from a man who truly believes nothing is sacred and intends to prove it. **104 pages $9**

BB-037 **"The Haunted Vagina" Carlton Mellick III** - It's difficult to love a woman whose vagina is a gateway to the world of the dead. **132 pages $10**

BB-042 **"Teeth and Tongue Landscape" Carlton Mellick III** - On a planet made out of meat, a socially-obsessive monophobic man tries to find his place amongst the strange creatures and communities that he comes across. **110 pages $10**

BB-043 **"War Slut" Carlton Mellick III** - Part "1984," part "Waiting for Godot," and part action horror video game adaptation of John Carpenter's "The Thing." **116 pages** **$10**

BB-045 **"Dr. Identity" D. Harlan Wilson** - Follow the Dystopian Duo on a killing spree of epic proportions through the irreal postcapitalist city of Bliptown where time ticks sideways, artificial Bug-Eyed Monsters punish citizens for consumer-capitalist lethargy, and ultraviolence is as essential as a daily multivitamin. **208 pages** **$15**

BB-047 **"Sausagey Santa" Carlton Mellick III** - A bizarro Christmas tale featuring Santa as a piratey mutant with a body made of sausages. 124 pages $10

BB-048 **"Misadventures in a Thumbnail Universe" Vincent Sakowski** - Dive deep into the surreal and satirical realms of neo-classical Blender Fiction, filled with television shoes and flesh-filled skies. **120 pages** **$10**

BB-049 **"Vacation" Jeremy C. Shipp** - Blueblood Bernard Johnson leaved his boring life behind to go on The Vacation, a year-long corporate sponsored odyssey. But instead of seeing the world, Bernard is captured by terrorists, becomes a key figure in secret drug wars, and, worse, doesn't once miss his secure American Dream. **160 pages** **$14**

BB-053 **"Ballad of a Slow Poisoner" Andrew Goldfarb** Millford Mutterwurst sat down on a Tuesday to take his afternoon tea, and made the unpleasant discovery that his elbows were becoming flatter. **128 pages** **$10**

BB-055 **"Help! A Bear is Eating Me" Mykle Hansen** - The bizarro, heartwarming, magical tale of poor planning, hubris and severe blood loss... **150 pages** **$11**

BB-056 **"Piecemeal June" Jordan Krall** - A man falls in love with a living sex doll, but with love comes danger when her creator comes after her with crab-squid assassins. **90 pages** **$9**

BB-058 "The Overwhelming Urge" Andersen Prunty - A collection of bizarro tales by Andersen Prunty. **150 pages $11**

BB-059 "Adolf in Wonderland" Carlton Mellick III - A dreamlike adventure that takes a young descendant of Adolf Hitler's design and sends him down the rabbit hole into a world of imperfection and disorder. **180 pages $11**

BB-061 "Ultra Fuckers" Carlton Mellick III - Absurdist suburban horror about a couple who enter an upper middle class gated community but can't find their way out. **108 pages $9**

BB-062 "House of Houses" Kevin L. Donihe - An odd man wants to marry his house. Unfortunately, all of the houses in the world collapse at the same time in the Great House Holocaust. Now he must travel to House Heaven to find his departed fiancee. **172 pages $11**

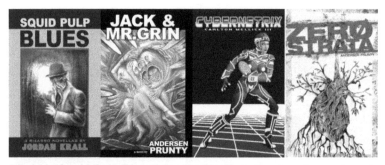

BB-064 "Squid Pulp Blues" Jordan Krall - In these three bizarro-noir novellas, the reader is thrown into a world of murderers, drugs made from squid parts, deformed gun-toting veterans, and a mischievous apocalyptic donkey. **204 pages $12**

BB-065 "Jack and Mr. Grin" Andersen Prunty - "When Mr. Grin calls you can hear a smile in his voice. Not a warm and friendly smile, but the kind that seizes your spine in fear. You don't need to pay your phone bill to hear it. That smile is in every line of Prunty's prose." - Tom Bradley. **208 pages $12**

BB-066 "Cybernetrix" Carlton Mellick III - What would you do if your normal everyday world was slowly mutating into the video game world from Tron? **212 pages $12**

BB-072 "Zerostrata" Andersen Prunty - Hansel Nothing lives in a tree house, suffers from memory loss, has a very eccentric family, and falls in love with a woman who runs naked through the woods every night. **144 pages $11**

BB-073 "The Egg Man" Carlton Mellick III - It is a world where humans reproduce like insects. Children are the property of corporations, and having an enormous ten-foot brain implanted into your skull is a grotesque sexual fetish. Mellick's industrial urban dystopia is one of his darkest and grittiest to date. **184 pages $11**

BB-074 "Shark Hunting in Paradise Garden" Cameron Pierce - A group of strange humanoid religious fanatics travel back in time to the Garden of Eden to discover it is invested with hundreds of giant flying maneating sharks. **150 pages $10**

BB-075 "Apeshit" Carlton Mellick III - Friday the 13th meets Visitor Q. Six hipster teens go to a cabin in the woods inhabited by a deformed killer. An incredibly fucked-up parody of B-horror movies with a bizarro slant. **192 pages $12**

BB-076 "Fuckers of Everything on the Crazy Shitting Planet of the Vomit At smosphere" Mykle Hansen - Three bizarro satires. Monster Cocks, Journey to the Center of Agnes Cuddlebottom, and Crazy Shitting Planet. **228 pages $12**

BB-077 "The Kissing Bug" Daniel Scott Buck - In the tradition of Roald Dahl, Tim Burton, and Edward Gorey, comes this bizarro anti-war children's story about a bohemian conenose kissing bug who falls in love with a human woman. **116 pages $10**

BB-078 "MachoPoni" Lotus Rose - It's My Little Pony... *Bizarro* style! A long time ago Poniworld was split in two. On one side of the Jagged Line is the Pastel Kingdom, a magical land of music, parties, and positivity. On the other side of the Jagged Line is Dark Kingdom inhabited by an army of undead ponies. **148 pages $11**

BB-079 "The Faggiest Vampire" Carlton Mellick III - A Roald Dahl-esque children's story about two faggy vampires who partake in a mustache competition to find out which one is truly the faggiest. **104 pages $10**

BB-080 "Sky Tongues" Gina Ranalli - The autobiography of Sky Tongues, the biracial hermaphrodite actress with tongues for fingers. Follow her strange life story as she rises from freak to fame. **204 pages $12**

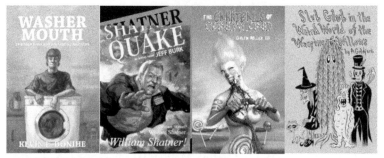

BB-081 **"Washer Mouth" Kevin L. Donihe** - A washing machine becomes human and pursues his dream of meeting his favorite soap opera star. **244 pages $11**

BB-082 **"Shatnerquake" Jeff Burk** - All of the characters ever played by William Shatner are suddenly sucked into our world. Their mission: hunt down and destroy the real William Shatner. **100 pages $10**

BB-083 **"The Cannibals of Candyland" Carlton Mellick III** - There exists a race of cannibals that are made of candy. They live in an underground world made out of candy. One man has dedicated his life to killing them all. **170 pages $11**

BB-084 **"Slub Glub in the Weird World of the Weeping Willows"** **Andrew Goldfarb** - The charming tale of a blue glob named Slub Glub who helps the weeping willows whose tears are flooding the earth. There are also hyenas, ghosts, and a voodoo priest **100 pages $10**

BB-085 **"Super Fetus" Adam Pepper** - Try to abort this fetus and he'll kick your ass! **104 pages $10**

BB-086 **"Fistful of Feet" Jordan Krall** - A bizarro tribute to spaghetti westerns, featuring Cthulhu-worshipping Indians, a woman with four feet, a crazed gunman who is obsessed with sucking on candy, Syphilis-ridden mutants, sexually transmitted tattoos, and a house devoted to the freakiest fetishes. **228 pages $12**

BB-087 **"Ass Goblins of Auschwitz" Cameron Pierce** - It's Monty Python meets Nazi exploitation in a surreal nightmare as can only be imagined by Bizarro author Cameron Pierce. **104 pages $10**

BB-088 **"Silent Weapons for Quiet Wars" Cody Goodfellow** - "This is high-end psychological surrealist horror meets bottom-feeding low-life crime in a techno-thrilling science fiction world full of Lovecraft and magic..." -John Skipp **212 pages $12**

BB-089 "Warrior Wolf Women of the Wasteland" Carlton Mellick III
Road Warrior Werewolves versus McDonaldland Mutants...post-apocalyptic fiction has never been quite like this. **316 pages $13**

BB-090 "Cursed" Jeremy C Shipp - The story of a group of characters who believe they are cursed and attempt to figure out who cursed them and why. A tale of stylish absurdism and suspenseful horror. **218 pages $15**

BB-091 "Super Giant Monster Time" Jeff Burk - A tribute to choose your own adventures and Godzilla movies. Will you escape the giant monsters that are rampaging the fuck out of your city and shit? Or will you join the mob of alien-controlled punk rockers causing chaos in the streets? What happens next depends on you. **188 pages $12**

BB-092 "Perfect Union" Cody Goodfellow - "Cronenberg's THE FLY on a grand scale: human/insect gene-spliced body horror, where the human hive politics are as shocking as the gore." -John Skipp. **272 pages $13**

BB-093 "Sunset with a Beard" Carlton Mellick III - 14 stories of surreal science fiction. **200 pages $12**

BB-094 "My Fake War" Andersen Prunty - The absurd tale of an unlikely soldier forced to fight a war that, quite possibly, does not exist. It's Rambo meets Waiting for Godot in this subversive satire of American values and the scope of the human imagination. **128 pages $11**

BB-095 "Lost in Cat Brain Land" Cameron Pierce - Sad stories from a surreal world. A fascist mustache, the ghost of Franz Kafka, a desert inside a dead cat. Primordial entities mourn the death of their child. The desperate serve tea to mysterious creatures. A hopeless romantic falls in love with a pterodactyl. And much more. **152 pages $11**

BB-096 "The Kobold Wizard's Dildo of Enlightenment +2" Carlton Mellick III - A Dungeons and Dragons parody about a group of people who learn they are only made up characters in an AD&D campaign and must find a way to resist their nerdy teenaged players and retarded dungeon master in order to survive. 232 **pages $12**

BB-097 **"My Heart Said No, but the Camera Crew Said Yes!" Bradley Sands** - A collection of short stories that are crammed with the delightfully odd and the scurrilously silly. **140 pages $13**

BB-098 **"A Hundred Horrible Sorrows of Ogner Stump" Andrew Goldfarb** - Goldfarb's acclaimed comic series. A magical and weird journey into the horrors of everyday life. **164 pages $11**

BB-099 **"Pickled Apocalypse of Pancake Island" Cameron Pierce** A demented fairy tale about a pickle, a pancake, and the apocalypse. **102 pages $8**

BB-100 **"Slag Attack" Andersen Prunty** - Slag Attack features four visceral, noir stories about the living, crawling apocalypse.A slag is what survivors are calling the slug-like maggots raining from the sky, burrowing inside people, and hollowing out their flesh and their sanity. **148 pages $11**

BB-101 **"Slaughterhouse High" Robert Devereaux** - A place where schools are built with secret passageways, rebellious teens get zippers installed in their mouths and genitals, and once a year, on that special night, one couple is slaughtered and the bits of their bodies are kept as souvenirs. **304 pages $13**

BB-102 **"The Emerald Burrito of Oz" John Skipp & Marc Levinthal** OZ IS REAL! Magic is real! The gate is really in Kansas! And America is finally allowing Earth tourists to visit this weird-ass, mysterious land. But when Gene of Los Angeles heads off for summer vacation in the Emerald City, little does he know that a war is brewing...a war that could destroy both worlds. **280 pages $13**

BB-103 **"The Vegan Revolution... with Zombies" David Agranoff** When there's no more meat in hell, the vegans will walk the earth. **160 pages $11**

BB-104 **"The Flappy Parts" Kevin L Donihe** - Poems about bunnies, LSD, and police abuse. You know, things that matter. **132 pages $11**

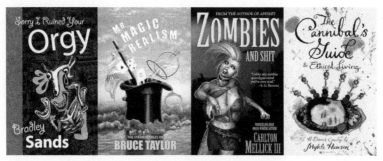

BB-105 **"Sorry I Ruined Your Orgy" Bradley Sands** - Bizarro humorist Bradley Sands returns with one of the strangest, most hilarious collections of the year. **130 pages $11**

BB-106 **"Mr. Magic Realism" Bruce Taylor** - Like Golden Age science fiction comics written by Freud, *Mr. Magic Realism* is a strange, insightful adventure that spans the furthest reaches of the galaxy, exploring the hidden caverns in the hearts and minds of men, women, aliens, and biomechanical cats. **152 pages $11**

BB-107 **"Zombies and Shit" Carlton Mellick III** - "Battle Royale" meets "Return of the Living Dead." Mellick's bizarro tribute to the zombie genre. **308 pages $13**

BB-108 **"The Cannibal's Guide to Ethical Living" Mykle Hansen** - Over a five star French meal of fine wine, organic vegetables and human flesh, a lunatic delivers a witty, chilling, disturbingly sane argument in favor of eating the rich.. **184 pages $11**

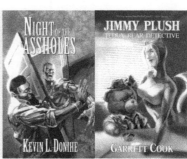

BB-109 **"Starfish Girl" Athena Villaverde** - In a post-apocalyptic underwater dome society, a girl with a starfish growing from her head and an assassin with sea anenome hair are on the run from a gang of mutant fish men. **160 pages $11**

BB-110 **"Lick Your Neighbor" Chris Genoa** - Mutant ninjas, a talking whale, kung fu masters, maniacal pilgrims, and an alcoholic clown populate Chris Genoa's surreal, darkly comical and unnerving reimagining of the first Thanksgiving. **303 pages $13**

BB-111 **"Night of the Assholes" Kevin L. Donihe** - A plague of assholes is infecting the countryside. Normal everyday people are transforming into jerks, snobs, dicks, and douchebags. And they all have only one purpose: to make your life a living hell.. **192 pages $11**

BB-112 **"Jimmy Plush, Teddy Bear Detective" Garrett Cook** - Hardboiled cases of a private detective trapped within a teddy bear body. **180 pages $11**

Lightning Source UK Ltd.
Milton Keynes UK
UKHW041836211118
332759UK00001B/68/P

9 781936 383894